The Keepers of the Balloon's Secret

J M Goode

For Poppy and Miriam

'Nothing seems really to matter, that's the charm of it. Whether you get away, or whether you don't; whether you arrive at your destination or whether you reach somewhere else, or whether you never get anywhere at all, you're always busy, and you never do anything in particular; and when you've done it there's always something else to do, and you can do it if you like, but you'd much better not.'

Ratty 'The Wind in the Willows'

'That's the thing with magic. You've got to know it is still here, all around us, or it just stays invisible for you.'

Charles de Lint

This is a story about treasure maps, lost castles, secret tunnels and old mysteries. It should have been told a long time ago but there was always something getting in the way.

Life plays a funny game of making things seem very busy when actually nothing really important is happening at all.

Sometimes we all need to stop and, when we do, it is when we see those little windows of peace and calm that remind us that the world we live in doesn't really have to be so busy. It is also stopping, that helps us see when the magic happens, and magic does happen all the time; you just have to look.

This adventure all started when Finn found a red balloon that was caught in a hedge at the corner of a field.

Chapter 1. A rather podgy balloon

It was one of those beautiful summer days. The days that make you feel warm inside even thinking about them in the darkest depths of winter. The days when there are no clouds, and the sky is as blue as you can ever imagine. Even if a cloud does try and appear, it soon vanishes back to where it came from, as if being told off by the sun. The kind of day when you look up, you feel that the sun is shining just for you. It was on a day like this that Finn was walking in a field near his family farm with his dog Rocket, when something caught his eye.

Finn trailed his hand in the warm knee length grass as it tickled his knees. He could see Rocket bouncing up and down, like a dolphin playing in a tropical sea. Every so often, Finn would lose sight of Rocket then a few moments later, Rocket would burst up into the air with what definitely looked like a smile. Finn and Rocket were best friends, and they made sure they did everything together.

A buzzard circled overhead and drifted up and up, in the warm thermals. The field Finn was walking in was enormous, it was so big, it was impossible to see from one end to the other. The land rolled up and down like a crinkled duvet of grass. It was perched on the side of a hill and he could see for miles around. Woodland backed onto the field and the farm track wiggled its way like a giant dusty worm through to the road half a mile away.

Finn loved walking in this field. He could see his farm below him and imagined his mum and dad busy with the cattle for milking. Summer was the best time, but each month gave him a different feeling as the seasons changed. Today, he imagined that he was an ancient king, leading his army over the hill and looking at the land in front of him as his new kingdom. Finn stood there leaning on his sword which was actually just a stick. But not just any stick, to Finn it was his special stick. He found it on a walk with his Dad and the second he picked it up, he knew it was made for him. He kept the stick in a corner in the kitchen and always took it out when he walked Rocket. It was also the perfect length to slash stinging nettles with, which came in handy when he kicked his football over the wall in the pigsties at the back of the farm.

Just then something caught Finn's attention. Something or someone was waving at him in the hedge at the corner of the field. He couldn't see what it was but knew straight away he had to get closer. The King and his army vanished; without a second thought he was bounding as best he could over the grass to the strange object.

It wasn't easy to run in the grass as it slowed him down and he couldn't get his legs moving properly. It was as if giant elastic bands were tied round his knees and pulling him backwards. Rocket's bounding technique was much more fun and, with his stick, Finn was able to plant it before him and bound even higher. This was what a proper adventurer would do he told himself.

Finn bounded across the field whooping in delight at the sheer excitement of it all.

Whatever Finn had seen changed from red to silver and then back to red again. It shimmered in the heat haze above the grass. As he bounded, he called out to Rocket who pricked up her ears and changed her course to follow her master.

Rocket was the fastest dog in the world according to Finn. When she was running really fast, her ears bent back against her head and that gave her super speed. Well, that's what Finn's father told him. When Finn was given her as a puppy, he had considered calling her Rocky Road as it was his favourite treat that Mum made him on his Birthday. After a lot of thinking, well, only about half an hour, but that's a lot of thinking time for a ten-year-old. Finn decided on Rocket. This also seemed to suit her much better and it would have looked a bit silly standing in the farmyard and calling out 'Rocky Road' really loudly.

Just then, Rocket whooshed past Finn's left leg and for a fraction of a second, Finn could feel the warmth of her body as she glided by him without even trying and disappeared into the long grass so the only thing you could see was the grass moving as Rocket hurtled towards the hedgerow.

'Hey that's not fair, I'm trying to run, I mean…. bound as fast as I can! You don't even know where we are heading to?' shouted Finn to Rocket as he got within throwing distance of the hedge.

Just at that point, Rocket stopped and Finn made one more gigantic bound and ended up with a Rocket cushioned landing in the grass. Laughing together, they rolled over and over, smothering the grass down, so it looked like a very fat cow had been sitting down, as they do just before it is going to rain.

'Rocky! You shouldn't stop so quickly!' said Finn as he sat up and gave her a gentle rub on the forehead. Rocket looked at him panting, a huge dog smile on her face and wagged her tail to say, 'Can we do that again?'

Finn was now close enough to see what it was that had caught his attention. Sitting quite ordinarily in the top branches of the hedge was one of those special red and silver balloons. I say a special one as it was not like a normal balloon that you pin up at home for special occasions. You know the one's that come in different shapes in a small packet and it hurts your ears if you try to blow them up. In fact, you're doing very well to blow them up at all and then you have the even more difficult task of tying a knot in it. It is unbelievably tricky, especially when you are a child, and the chances are you get your fingers stuck in the knot which makes them go very red and you have to ask an adult for help.

This balloon was one of those special shiny ones that fly all by themselves. The ones they sell at summer fairs or in crowded high streets at Christmas. They float and hover above everyone's heads, moving in a very lazy, sluggish way. The balloon in the top of the hedge had clearly been popped on the branches as it was only half full of air. It gave the impression of a sad old man in a red cardigan who had eaten too much for dinner and was sat in an armchair at a peculiar angle. It made Finn think of evil Farmer Cramner who lived on a farm a few fields away. He had once caught Finn 'snooping' around. This was not true as Finn had only gone a short way into a field to try and find his Frisbee, when it had gone too far from a very wild throw. The kind of throw that would definitely have set a world record but sadly no one was there to see it apart from him and Rocket. Farmer Cramner had shouted at Finn to get off his land and had even phoned Finn's father to tell him about what happened. Ever since then, Finn had stayed clear of him, but this red balloon reminded him of Farmer Cramner's big belly, and it was the same colour as the waistcoat he always seemed to wear.

The hedgerow was taller than he remembered, and the balloon was caught right at the top of it. Finn stood up and reached up with his stick. He could just about touch the balloon and move it a small amount with a waggle of the stick. It was then that Finn noticed the balloon had something tied to the bottom of it. What was it? It seemed to be some sort of note that was held onto the balloon with string. Finn tried his hardest to dislodge the balloon but even though he was sure he was jumping higher than he ever had before, he just couldn't move it. Looking around him he realised that he needed a longer stick.

'Rocket stay here and guard the balloon, I'm going to the woods to see if I can find a branch, we can use to hook the balloon off the hedge with,' said Finn.

It wasn't long before Finn was scuttling around in the undergrowth at the edge of the wood to see what he could find. He made sure he stayed within leaping distance of the field, just in case, the woods were always a mysterious place to go. Finn always wanted to explore them more and wished he was that little bit braver. The woods got darker the further you went in. His mother had warned him about getting lost in the woods.

'It all looks the same once you're lost, you don't know which way to turn' his mother had said.

There would be strange sounds and it was always as if someone was watching you from behind one of the old trees. What secrets did they hold? Once when he was feeling really brave he ran in so far it was almost dark around him when he stopped, the trees were blocking out the light and there was a strange spongy coloured moss on the floor. He then ran faster than he had ever run before to make it back out into the sunlight and safety of the fields. His heart was beating so fast and he promised himself that he was not going to be quite so brave again for a long time.

At last, Finn found a long branch that had been broken off one of the trees in a recent storm. He snapped a few loose branches off it and proudly strode out towards the obedient Rocket with his new invention.'

The 'super balloon saving device' proclaimed Finn as if he were one of the greatest inventors in the world. It had a forked prong at the top which would make it perfect for hooking the balloon off to safety. It had also crossed Finn's mind that his new branch could make a handy pole vault. Not that he had ever done the pole vault, but he had seen it on the TV at the last Olympics and reasoned that with a bit of practice he would be quite good at it. Suddenly he heard Rocket give a low growl.

'What is it Rocky?' said Finn.

Rocket continued to growl and Finn turned to see what was bothering her. It wasn't like Rocket to growl as she was normally such a happy dog and she very rarely barked. Standing at the edge of the wood where Finn had just come from stood Farmer Cramner.

He was wearing old Wellington boots that looked like he hadn't taken them off in months. Rumpled around his legs were dirty green corduroyed trousers. He had no belt on and his fat belly was hanging out under his shirt and red waist coat. The bottom few buttons of his shirt were missing as they had clearly lost the battle against his belly, which meant his hairy bulging stomach was on show for all to see all the time. Despite it being a summer day, he was wearing his faded green corduroyed jacket that matched his trousers. There were holes in his elbows and his sleeves looked worn and stringy. On his cauliflower shaped head, he wore a crumpled black hat that was too small and his white straw hair was poking out in all directions. He had a big red shiny nose and stubbly salt and pepper cheeks. The sort only long-lost aunties seems to have perfected. One eye was half open and his buck teeth were obvious as he performed some sort of weird snarl directed at Finn.

Finn was stuck rooted to the spot. His knees trembled and suddenly the day didn't feel quite so warm. This was the first time he had seen Farmer Cramner since the Frisbee incident and he had been worried about meeting him ever since. Had he done anything wrong? He wasn't sure who owned the woods but would he really be in trouble for taking a branch that was already on the floor? How long had he been there?

'Get of my land boy' gurgled Farmer Cramner in a rustic drawl. He was shaking his fist and each time he did, his belly wobbled below his shirt.

Finn didn't know what to say or do. Did he really say get 'of' his land? It did cross Finn's mind to inform Farmer

Cramner that the word he should have used was 'off' not 'of,' but he did not think that would go down very well at that precise moment. Just to confirm to Finn that he had not misheard him, Farmer Cramner gave another round of, 'Get of my land' with even more urgency and as a result a stronger degree of belly wobbled to and fro.

'Yes, Sir', stammered Finn.

'Sorry, I was just looking for a branch'. At which point, Finn half-heartedly held up the balloon saving device to prove what he was saying was true. Cramner gave him an even more puzzled stare and made a strangely rude noise. Looking back on it, Finn realised the noise could have only been one thing. After the noise had finished which seemed to take a least ten seconds, Farmer Cramner shook his fist once more and then turned his back and hobbled back into the undergrowth of the woods.

Finn let out a long breath and looked at Rocket who had her head tilted sideways at him.

'Oh Rocky, I wish you could talk and help me tell Mum and Dad what just happened, I really hope he doesn't call up Dad for a second time, I don't think I've done anything wrong?

The sun felt warm again and the birds seemed to find their song as a gentle breeze rustled the balloon. All of a sudden, Farmer Cramner's visit to the edge of the field was forgotten as Finn turned his attention to getting the balloon down.

It didn't take long for Finn to work out how to use his new branch to hook itself onto the string and Finn was proudly lifting the balloon and its note off the hedge. As Finn held the branch with its prize on top a fresh gust of wind caught the balloon and it soared off the branch back up into the air.

'Oh no!' cried Finn as he could see the balloon drifting up and off out of his reach.

'Quick, Rocket follow that balloon, we can't let it get away.'

Finn dropped the branch and grabbed his special stick before he started to bound after the balloon through the grass. Rocket was doing her best to follow it in the air but could not get the idea of running with her head up. Whenever she looked up at the balloon she had to stop and then start again when she realised where it was. The balloon looked like it was making one last effort to find a new resting place where it couldn't be disturbed. The warm air was swirling it around, up and down. Despite it not having a lot of air left, it was still doing its best to fly up and away. Finn was chasing at full sprint and the further it got away from him the more desperate he was to catch it. He was like a fish being toyed with as he changed course this way and that across the green pond of a field.

Finally, the balloon seemed to give up to its fate and it began to sink down towards earth. Finn saw his chance and sprinted that little bit faster to make sure it wasn't going to escape him again. Just at the last second as Finn was about to jump up and take hold of the note and string, Rocket leapt from what must have been a dog's long jump record to soar through the air above Finn and snatch the balloon in her teeth. For the second time that day, Rocket and Finn found themselves rolling in the grass together. This time they had the strange balloon and its even stranger note attached to it.

Chapter 2. A mysterious note

Finn knelt in the grass and took hold of the note. It was slightly faded as the ink had run a bit due to it being out in open. Finn looked puzzled and stared at the note. He read it again. It wasn't what he was expecting. If he was honest, I do not think he knew what he expected to be written on a note attached to a balloon. This was the first one he had ever found. The note had only one sentence but those few words made the hairs on Finn's neck stand up. He shook his head and then read the words out to Rocket as if speaking them aloud would make them easier to understand. Rocket was doing her tilted head thing and looking as if she was doing her best to understand. The note simply said this:

'You have found the balloon, now you need to find the map which will lead you to the treasure. Look to where people study in Buckland Farm.'
Signed   A

Finn couldn't believe it. He kept staring at the note and half expected someone to come running up and say it was all a joke, but the field remained empty and, all of a sudden, he had a feeling that something very special was going to happen. This was the start of a proper adventure. The very thought of going after the treasure map gave him goose bumps on his arms and his tummy felt all knotted, his eyebrows seemed to have moved a couple of inches up his forehead as he took in what he had found. He had found a note telling him of a treasure map.

Straight away Finn wondered what he should do next. Should he tell his mum and dad? He didn't have any brothers and sisters to share it with as he was an only child. He could tell his friends from school, but would they believe him? His best friend Toby lived a few roads away and Finn knew that Toby would love to hear about what he had found. He just was not sure what to do or who to tell. As if Rocket was able to read his mind she gave a small bark to reassure Finn that she was there. Finn looked up from the note and laughed lightly at her.

'Of course, Rocky, I know you are with me. We do not need to tell anyone about this just yet. We can see if we can find the map together,' said Finn resting his hand on Rocket's head and feeling the softness of her ears. Rocket liked this and gave him a big lick on the side of the cheek.

'Uurggh Rocket,' said Finn as he got to his feet and rubbed his face with the back of his hand.

'Now, let's head back home as it's time we should be getting back. Mum will be wondering where we have got to.' Finn safely tucked the note into his pocket and scrunched the balloon up into the other one. He went over the words on it again in his head as he strode leisurely down the hill to his farm with Rocket at his side.

Apart from all the excitement, the only thing that was troubling him was that the note mentioned Buckland Farm. He knew where it was, but Buckland Farm was the one place he didn't want to go. It was an abandoned old farm and he had been told it was extremely dangerous.

At school, he had heard children say it was haunted and no one had been there in years. His father had warned him never to go there. Only once had Finn been to the gateway of the farm track when he and Toby were riding around on the lanes on their bikes. They had looked up the drive to see the deserted farm buildings shrouded in a strange damp mist. It seemed to rest on the floor around the farmhouse like a patchy white dress. The windows were dark holes with no glass left and old ragged bits of curtains hung limply like a witch's haircut. Everything in the house looked black and scary. There was an eerie feeling as the rooks, high up in their nests squawked at them, telling them to stay away. He and Toby had not hung around, they quickly turned and peddled away extremely fast.

'It can't be that bad Rocky, I'm not going to let a few stories put me off finding the treasure map. Anyway, nothing great is easy. Well, that's what Uncle Mike tells me,' said Finn as turned the gate to enter his farmyard.

Chickens scooted this way and that as Rocket jumped towards them. Rocket knew not to harm them, but she couldn't help herself having a bit of fun with them.

'Rocket, no, stop that. You know you're not meant to scare the chickens, come here and get a drink, you must be so thirsty. Thinking about it, I need a big drink too.'

Finn opened the door to the farmhouse to be met by the delicious smell of his mother's cooking. He checked his pocket one last time to see the note was still there. One thing occurred to him that he hadn't really thought about. The note was signed with a capital A. Finn wondered what on earth that could mean. He didn't know of anyone with a letter A at the beginning of their name. Perhaps he could ask his mum and dad at supper subtly if they knew anyone around here with an A at the start of their name. If he could work out who A was then that might shed some light as to what and where the treasure was?

The next thing he had to work out was when he was going to visit Buckland Farm. When would be the best time to go? Would he be seen by someone if he went in the daytime? Was it too risky? Did that mean the only option was for him to go at night-time? It almost made his knees go weak just at the thought.

Whatever Finn decided, he knew he was going to have to be brave to find the treasure map in Buckland Farm. It might be the scariest thing in the world, but he was going to do it.

At dinner, he had tried to ask his mum and dad whether they knew anyone whose name started with the letter A. They both looked at him and stopped eating, confusion written all over their faces. Finn realised he had to change the subject quickly otherwise they would work out that he was up to something.

'I wonder if a panda has ever met a penguin' said Finn. Both his parents looked at each other before turning their gaze back to him.

'That's a very strange thing to say dear,' said his mum, 'Where did that come from?'

'Oh, I was just wondering' said Finn, going a little rosy in the cheeks. What on earth did he say that for? It was the first thing that came into his head. There then proceeded to be that awkward silence where all that can be heard is the uncomfortable noise of knife and forks and plates being scraped and people chewing. Thankfully, it did not last long, as the silence was broken by a loud squawk from outside in the yard.

'Those chickens! Do you think its Rocket playing with them again?' said his mum.

'She'd better not be,' said his father, 'Anyway someone needs to go and close their hutch for the night'.

'I'll do it' said Finn, 'Thanks for supper Mum, it was perfect.' Finn got up and kissed his mother on the cheek before dashing out the door and calling for Rocket. His parents looked at each other and gave a brief shake of their heads.

Finn couldn't sleep that night, he kept thinking about what the note said and whether he could actually find the map. He lay in bed looking at the stars through his open window. He loved the night sky and listened out for all the nocturnal sounds that would drift in over his thoughts. The distant noise of fox barking somewhere far away. An owl hooting up in the woods. It was as if the owl was calling to him and telling him something urgent. If only he could understand what it was saying?

Down the corridor, he could hear the rumbling rhythm of his dad snoring which he was so used to. Thank goodness he was a few rooms away. His mum had to wear ear plugs to stop the noise disturbing her! Even the creaky floorboards didn't wake them when Finn padded his sleepy walk to the use the loo in the night.

Just then, he had an idea. It was one of those ideas that suddenly hit you between the eyes and you know straight away that whatever it is you have to go with it. He sat up in bed wide awake and buzzing with excitement. This was it; he was going to go to Buckland Farm tonight. Right now! He had already thought it would be too risky to visit in the day as he could be seen by someone. He would go now and take a torch and Rocket for safety. It would only take about ten minutes to cycle there. He knew the way and the moon was so bright it would be easy to see.

Finn quickly got dressed into the same clothes being very careful not to tread on the floorboards that made extra-loud creaky noises. He was well practised as sometimes at Christmas he would see if he could tip toe all the way along the corridor and back again without waking up any of his relatives when they came to stay. He had worked out there is something very exciting about creeping slowly somewhere trying not to be heard by anyone.

Finn used all his silent stealth to make it downstairs, step by step. He didn't think his parents would wake up as his dad's snoring was so loud. The hard bit would be opening the back door. The house was silent apart from the distant rumble upstairs. The kitchen looked very different in the dark. He knew it so well, but at night-time, it always made things that were familiar seem strange. Rocket looked up from her basket as if she had been expecting him. She nuzzled her wet nose into his hand and her tail wagged sleepily against the table leg. Finn bent down and put his finger to his lips to show Rocket there was to be no noise. As if Rocket understood, she bowed her head and her tail stopped the brushing noise against the table.

Finn tip toed around the kitchen and handily found his favourite blue jumper on the back of a chair, which he tied around his waist. He crept to the dresser and opened the draw that was always full of things that didn't have anywhere else to live. There were batteries, pens, a box of matches, a random glove, postcards, old keys, elastic bands, a few old coins and other random small objects that he had no idea what they were for. He carefully dug out a small black torch that had been in there forever. His trainers were by the back door and Finn did that special wobbly leg trick of slipping his feet into them without having to untie the laces.

This was the moment he had to get right when he opened the back door. He had thought about jumping out a kitchen window but realised he wouldn't be able to get back in so easily. Also how would he get Rocket out of the window without waking his parents up? He slowly turned the key in the lock, squinting at Rocket with his teeth clenched. Finn held his breath as he felt that might make a difference. The lock clicked and sounded like a gun had gone off in the kitchen. The seconds passed and there was no movement from upstairs. He had done it. The handle turned smoothly, and he was able to gently open the door to feel the cool night air waft around his legs.

The moonlight lit up the farmyard, it always amazed Finn how bright the night could be. Everything was very still and peaceful as if a big blanket of sleep had been spread across the farm. He could hear the cattle lowing in the barn and the noises of the foxes and owls in the woods. Finn gave a shudder of fear when he thought about going into the woods at night, but then he remembered what he was doing now and his trip to Buckland Farm was going to be just as scary.

Was this a good idea after all? Perhaps it would be best to wait until the daytime he thought to himself? What if his parents were to wake up and check on him and find he wasn't there? Then he would be in serious trouble and the new bike he was hoping to get for his birthday would definitely not happen.

As always Rocket seemed to make the decision for him as she padded across the yard to where his bike was leaning against the wall. She turned around and gave him one of those looks that seemed to say, 'Come on!'

Chapter 3. Buckland Farm

Finn peddled so quickly his wheels spun like a washing machine. Rocket did what she did best and zoomed along with her tongue hanging out. He knew the quiet country roads well and the clear night sky made the journey easy. Finn remembered how for some reason you always feel like you go so much quicker at night when you run. He hadn't ridden his bike before when it was dark, and he felt so fast, hurtling along the lanes. He tried to not think what his parents would say about him riding around the roads without a bike light or his helmet on. He had never done anything like this, but he knew what he felt inside, and it was just something he had to do. He had to find the treasure map. What a strange few hours it had been but, ever since he had set eyes on the balloon, he was living an adventure.

Finn and Rocket were lit up by the moon as they wound their way through the lanes. The thick hedges on either side of the road were like dark green walls of carpet. Up above an owl glided past them, swiftly and silently. As he cycled, he had been thinking about what it meant on the note when it said, 'Look to where people study in Buckland Farm.' Did Buckland Farm used to be a school in the old days? Is that what it meant? Perhaps it means one of the rooms is a study and that's where the map is?

Eventually Finn arrived at the gateway of Buckland Farm and pulled up hesitantly.

Finn stared at the empty farm buildings and gave a big gulp. He looked down at Rocket for encouragement, Rocket stood there panting looking like she was having a brilliant time, with her tongue lolling out of her mouth. The track that led up to the farm had a line of scrubby grass in the middle, making it look like a giant furry caterpillar. The still night meant not a sound could be heard. This was it. He knew there was no going back now. Even though he was as scared as he had ever been, he had to go and try to find the map, it was somewhere in there.

Finn walked his bike down the track, and he could feel his skin tightening, the hairs on his legs stood on end as he got closer to the farm buildings. The cool night air swirled around him and brought a shiver to his body. The moonlight lit up the deserted farmyard and Finn thought how different it looked from where he lived. The farmhouse looked menacing as it stood before him in silence. The gaping black holes of the windows and doorway looked darker than anything he had ever seen.

Old, rusted farm machinery was scattered in the corners of the yard covered in thick blanket of sharp brambles and stinging nettles. There was strange smell hovering all around. Finn ever so slowly rested his bike against an old tractor tyre. This was not very much fun anymore and he felt he has left all his bravery at the top of the driveway.

Just then something flew at him out of the barn doorway. It skimmed above his head and Finn ducked in surprise and fear. The bat circled the farmyard and carried on its journey into the fields. Finn let out a deep breath very slowly. He had seen bats countless times before but that had seriously scared him. He tried to stop his leg shaking by pushing his foot into the ground hard. He couldn't give up now.

As Finn made his way towards the farmhouse doorway, he looked back and waved at Rocket to follow him. Rocket stood still and didn't budge an inch. She was giving him a very funny look. Why didn't Rocket move and come with him? What was it that made her stop and refuse to come into the farm? Without looking back, Finn took the torch from his pocket and stepped up into the blackness of the doorway. The smell hit him first, the damp dank green smell of decay. Finn's wobbly torch shone into the room as he stood there in the doorframe. The moonlight shone through the scraggy witch's hair curtains, illuminating the room in a ghostly way. The room was empty with strange marks on the walls. Dirt and mouse poo were scattered all over the broken tiled floor. It looked like no one had been here for years.

Finn moved forward, taking his steps slowly and surely. He ducked slightly in case any more bats would be startled by his entrance and swoop down on him. He held the torch in both hands to make it steadier, he was so nervous his whole body was shaking uncontrollably. There was nothing obvious to say that the treasure map would be in that room. He had to go further into the building.

Step by step he made his way across the room to the next doorway. The witch's hair curtains fluttered as he moved through the room. His feet crunched on the broken tiles. As he turned the corner to look, he could see a staircase across the far side of the next room and for some reason knew he had to climb it. The second room was much like the first. Nothing was in it apart from dirt and distant memories.

Suddenly Finn heard something. He could hear a noise. It was very faint but seemed to be getting louder. It sounded like a person whining. What was it? Where was it coming from? Was it upstairs? He turned around quickly, and the torch shone, lighting up all parts of the room. There was nothing there, but he could still hear the noise. It seemed to be getting louder and Finn was becoming more panicky. He should go back. This just wasn't safe or fun. Who cares if he quit now, it wouldn't matter? No one would know. The whining noise got louder and louder, something was here, someone was here.

Finn felt a cold bead of sweat drip down his forehead. This really was the scariest thing he had ever experienced. The whining noise stopped as suddenly as it had started, and everything was silent again.

From somewhere deep inside him, Finn found the courage to keep heading towards the staircase. He looked up at the rickety set of stairs and took another deep breath. The stairs creaked in pain under his weight and he only hoped they wouldn't collapse. Stair by stair he climbed up into the darkness. His torch was doing its best to light his way, but Finn had that horrible feeling that the batteries were starting to fade. If only he had checked the batteries when he had first taken it out of the draw. He had to speed up and find this map, wherever it could be?

The upstairs of the farmhouse felt darker and the moonlight couldn't be seen so easily. The old wallpaper had been torn off in patches, like a monster had walked along the corridor ripping parts of the wall with its claws. Mysterious doorways stood like gravestones as Finn shone his weakening torch down to the end room.

There, he could see something. At the end of the corridor, straight ahead of him was a room with something in it. It was the first piece of furniture he had found in the whole house. Could it be a table? Could this be where the treasure map was hidden? The moon had managed to shine a thin beam into the room giving enough light for Finn to see the object. With a newfound sense of purpose and the fact that his torch was definitely not going to last much longer, Finn strode along the corridor trying not to think what lay in the dark rooms he passed. His footsteps swirled the dust around his shoes as if he was walking through the morning mist of one of his father's fields.

And then it happened. His torch went out.

Finn was left in complete darkness apart from the few scattered moon beams that hung sadly through the windows. Fear prickled him all over and he could hear his heart beating loudly in his chest. So loud that he barely could hear anything apart from the thump, thump, thump of blood pumping in his ears. He kept walking towards the end room. His footsteps echoed around the empty farmhouse and the floorboards moaned with each movement.

The object that had caught Finn's attention was becoming clearer to him. His eyes were adjusting, and he could make out what he saw was an old child's writing desk. He had seen one before in a museum he had visited with school. It stood in the middle of the room, the rest of which was empty.

The desk had a lid to lift up and it was slightly sloped with an ink well in one corner. There were names and writing gauged into the wood made by children long ago. Names and words that Finn couldn't understand but one thing stood out to him and he squinted and moved closer to see it in the dim light. Someone had scratched a drawing of a dragon breathing fire into the top right-hand corner of the desk. The dragon looked like it was at the gates of a castle surrounded by trees. In the silence and stillness, Finn looked at the picture and wondered why anyone would take time to engrave such a scene. Had whoever drawn it seen this dragon? How long ago was this from?

So many things were going round his head. He tried to think clearly, 'This is a writing desk and it's where children worked, where people would study in Buckland Farm. This must be it. This is where the treasure map was hidden.'

Without hesitating Finn went to lift up the lid of the desk. Nothing happened to start with, and Finn feared it was locked. He tried again, very slowly he could feel the lid moving upwards. The dust cascaded down as the lid rose higher and the hinges let out a screeching noise that pierced the silence as if the desk was screaming at him.

Finn looked down into the compartment under the lid to find it was empty apart from a leather-bound black book. There was no writing on the cover and from what Finn could see it was old and worn. Finn reached down and took hold of the book. As soon as he had it in his hand the silence was broken by the strange wailing, whining noise. What was going on? By him moving the book, had this made the noise start? He felt fear grip him once more as the mysterious whining wound its ways towards him along the ghostly corridor. This was what they had talked about in school when they said Buckland Farm was haunted. This horrible noise must be the ghost and Finn had disturbed it. He had to get out now. He didn't want to see any kind of ghost! He didn't believe in them before but now this noise was making every hair on his body stand on end and fear was pounding through him.

Finn grabbed the book in both hands and made for the door of the room. He didn't look back and rushed down the corridor past the graveyard of black rooms. The noise was louder than ever before, it sounded horrendous, Finn could feel tears prick the corner of his eyes as he just wanted to get out into the open and be away from this place.

Whatever or whoever it was, was downstairs. The wailing noise rose up the stair case. In panic, Finn nearly tripped down the stairs and only at the last second did he stop himself from falling by slamming his hand onto the wooden rail. The rotten bannister gave away and it smashed onto the floor below sending clouds of dust shimmering in the moon light. Finn still had to get down the stairs, with tears streaming down his face and his body wracked with worry as to what waited for him at the bottom. Finn climbed down being careful not to let go of the black book.

The noise was coming from the first room he had entered. He had no way of getting out except through the door he came in by. Finn had to face whatever it was a few feet away. The noise was a screeching, whining, deathly wail. He moved closer to the door leading to the first room and plucked up all the courage he could find to take the next few steps. It was as if his body refused to move forward.

He edged himself to the door frame and peered into the darkness shaking. The horrendous noise stopped.

Rocket looked at him and gave a small, contented mewing noise. Her tail wagged and she did that funny thing with her ears where they stand on end and her head tilted to the side.

'ROCKET, I CAN'T BELIEVE YOU! IT WAS YOU ALL ALONG MAKING THAT HORRIBLE NOISE! YOU SCARED ME SO MUCH ROCKY, I AM SO GLAD IT WAS ONLY YOU.' with that Finn sank to his knees and cuffed away the tears from his cheeks.

Rocket wagged her way over to him and Finn gave her a huge hug as Rocket nuzzled herself into Finn's shoulder. All the fear and worry were draining from him as he realised what had happened. Poor Rocket had obviously heard him moving around the farmhouse and was scared herself.

'Oh Rocky, I'm so glad there wasn't a ghost down here, I haven't been so scared in all my life. It's amazing what your imagination can do when you start hearing strange noises,' said Finn.

'Look, I've found what we were looking for. This book must be what the note was taking about.' As if Rocket understood, she gave a small yap of excitement and smiled her doggy smile.

Finn made his way out into the farmyard. He couldn't believe how bright the moon was, as it lit up the way in front of him. He had the book safely in his hands. He so badly wanted to look in it, but knew he had to get away from Buckland Farm before anything else happened. He promised himself he would never, ever, go back in there again. A few minutes ago he was feeling so scared, but now, he was filled with excitement at the thought of what the book in his hands could reveal.

Finn peddled his bike down the path and held onto the handlebars with one hand. He had practised this many times and could even ride with no hands on a straight flat bit of road. The book was pressed firmly into his chest with his other arm and he wasn't going to let it go. Rocket lolloped along stopping to sniff something interesting before running to catch him.

He had no idea what time it was and he prayed his parents were still safely tucked up in bed with his dad snoring loudly. At the end of the drive, Finn gave a small smile of relief as he saw the tarmac road which would lead him home. He turned and waited for Rocket to catch him up; the excitement was all too much, he had to have a look in the book. He rested the book on the handlebars and opened the front cover.

Even though it was the middle of the night, the bright moon meant Finn could see what he needed to. It was not what Finn was expecting at all. The old book wasn't a proper book any way. Not like the ones you find in churches or libraries. The book had no pages in it. The pages had a square cut out of them, so only the outside of the pages were left. It was a secret book with a secret compartment. In the square space where the pages were meant to be, was a crusty yellow piece of folded paper. Finn's heart skipped a beat and the reality of what he was about to discover fizzled right through him.

Holding his breath, Finn lifted the piece of paper out of the book and unfolded it very carefully. The ancient paper was so fragile, he didn't want to rip it in his excitement. Rocket gave a whimper as if she knew this was a special moment.

Finn unfolded the paper to reveal a treasure map. This was the treasure map he had imagined. The map he had been scared witless to find. He held it in his hands and this time his hands shook with both excitement and anticipation.

The map showed paths and farms and places Finn knew. It had his own farm just below the fold in the paper. He could see the woods behind his house where Farmer Cramner had shouted at him. The river was marked that flowed at the bottom of the valley. Around the edges of the map were strange symbols that Finn didn't understand. There was something written along the bottom, but it was just too dark to read what it said. One corner of the map was torn, and Finn had to be careful not to make the tear worse, as he handled it. But the thing that made Finn's heart miss a beat for the second time that evening was the big thick black cross marked in the middle of the map. The cross was on top of a castle that had been drawn with towers and turrets and around the castle were trees. Finn could not believe it. His mind raced at the possibilities of what this meant. Could he find the treasure by himself? Did he need to tell someone?

Finn looked up at the night's sky as if the stars would have the answers to his questions. He glanced back down at the map. The first time he looked at it, he had not properly understood, but now he did.

A shiver of excitement ran through his body. The castle marked on the map was to be found in the woods behind his farm. This meant, the treasure was in the castle in the woods behind his farm. Finn knew this adventure was only just starting. He was going to do everything he possibly could to find the castle and then the treasure.

Chapter 4. Someone's coming

Finn blew into his cheeks when he realised what this meant. He couldn't believe it. Once more he felt the thrill of excitement course through his body. This was the most exciting night of his life!

Just then, Rocket's ear picked up and Finn knew straight away that she had heard something he could not. Rocket turned her head to the road and gave a low growl. Immediately Finn understood that he had to hide. He folded the paper as carefully as he could and placed it back into the book. As soon as he had done so, bright headlights appeared on the other side of the hill. A car was driving along the road and was going to pass right next to him and see him. He couldn't let this happen.

'Rocket, come on,' Finn urgently hissed, and he wheeled his bike into the field next to the farm track. Thankfully the grass hadn't been cut and he pressed himself down as flat as he could holding his arm over Rocket who put her paws out and watched from the long grass with her nose resting on the ground. The car wouldn't see them if they both stayed still. Finn prayed that it was going to drive straight by so he could get back on his bike and ride home as quickly as possible. For the first time, Finn realised the bright moon was now working against him as someone could see him if they stopped for long enough.

A thought had come into his mind that it was his father out looking for him. But how would he know he had cycled to Buckland Farm? He hadn't told anyone. No, he reassured himself, the car lights coming towards his hiding place would be no one he knew, and they would drive straight past. It must be someone who is lost driving around these lanes in the middle of the night.

The car headlights got brighter and brighter as the car made its way along the lane towards his hiding place. Finn pushed his head down into the grass to stop himself losing his night vision. He also thought this might help him remain even stiller if his head was down. Finn's heart began to beat faster again as he realised from the noise of the car that it was slowing down. He didn't move a muscle. The car engine ticked over directly next to them in the field. Whoever it was could have been looking right at them.

The car edged forward a small way. The noise of the engine echoed in Finn's ears, he dare not look up in case he was seen. They must be looking right at him, why else would the car stop?

The car then turned off the road onto the track for Buckland Farm. Finn turned his head to the side very slowly to see if he could see anything. Why was the car driving down to the deserted farm? What was it doing at this time of night? Was the person driving it also looking for something? Could they know about the treasure map as well?

Finn very gently lifted his head. The vehicle had moved slowly forward and was making its way towards Buckland Farm. Finn could see it was old clapped out Land Rover chugging down the drive. He was pretty sure Rocket and he hadn't been spotted but it must have been close. Thank goodness for the long grass and Rocket lying so still. As Finn picked up his bike, he knew he had to get onto the road and as far away from Buckland Farm as quick as he could. He took one last look down the drive at the land rover and Finn was sure that the silhouetted head of the driver he could see had the same small black hat and wiry scraggy hair as Farmer Cramner.

It didn't take Finn long to get home. A mixture of excitement and nerves fuelled his body and journeys always seem to go quicker on the way back. When he entered his own farmyard everything was quiet and the same as when he had left it. He tiptoed around to the back door and slipped inside with barely a sound. Rocket went to her bed in the corner of the kitchen. He could hear his father's snoring grumbling along like an old tractor. This helped him up the stairs as he only moved a stair when the snore was in full throttle.

At last Finn was able to collapse into his bed but not before he had placed the black leather-bound book and its secret under his pillow. He stared out of the window at the stars and gave a triumphant grin with what he had achieved that night. He realised this adventure was only just beginning and with that sleep folded its arms around him and he drifted off dreaming of castles in the woods.

Chapter 5. An unwelcome guest

'OH FINNY!......FINNY!.......FINN, WAKE UP SLEEPY HEAD', shouted his mum from downstairs in the kitchen.

'Do you want some lunch? You've been asleep for hours. Come downstairs, there's someone to see you'.

Finn woke up with a start. He had been in the middle of an amazing dream where he was a knight in armour defending his castle from an invading army. What time was it? The sun was already high in the sky. The farmyard noises and smells drifted in through the window. As he sat up in bed, he had to shield his eyes from the sun light and suddenly all that happened at Buckland Farm flooded back to him. He quickly spun around and pushed his hand under his pillow. He could feel the soft leather of the book and slowly pulled it out to see for certain that he hadn't imagined it.

The book looked even older and dirtier in the day light. It also gave off a musty smell that Finn hadn't noticed last night. He opened the cover to reveal the secret compartment with the treasure map folded where Finn had left it.

'What's that?' asked a girl of his age who was standing in the doorway.

Finn, taken completely by surprise, gave a small scream and stuffed the book under his duvet.

'Aarrghhh ….J... Je....Jess...Jessica, what on earth are you doing here? Said a completely flustered Finn.

He hadn't heard anyone come up the stairs and he must have been so sleepy and distracted by his treasure book that he had missed her footsteps.

'What's that book? It looks really old. Why have you hidden it?' said Jess as she moved into the room.

'What book?' said Finn trying to act as if nothing had happened.

'The book you just had in your hand and then stuffed under the duvet' said Jess looking at him accusingly.

Finn changed tact and went for a diversion.

'Hang on a minute Jess, you just can't walk in here and start asking questions! I was asleep two minutes ago. What are you doing here anyway? said Finn.

Jess wasn't going to give up. 'I'll tell you that when you tell me what the book is, it must be something secret, otherwise you wouldn't have hidden it.' 'Nice pyjamas by the way, who goes to bed in their shorts and t-shirt?'

'Secret....no, nothing secret. It's....it's... it's nothing' said Finn as he shook his head and tried his best to make it look like it really was nothing. He realised with a sinking feeling that Jess would not let this go and it was going to be very difficult not to tell her what it was.

Jess gave him a coy look and squinted her eyes at him. 'Well, whatever it is, we both know that you're going to tell me at some point today or tomorrow or even the next day, don't we Finlay? said Jess folding her arms and looking down at him from the end of her nose.

45

'What, what do you mean, today, tomorrow or even the next day?' said Finn.

He hated it when people called him by his full name. It was normally only used by his mother when she was frustrated with him, which wasn't very often, or on those strange occasions when he met relatives he hadn't seen in ages and they had said something along the lines of.

'Ah, look at you FINLAY, haven't you grown, why don't you come and give your Auntie Ethal a big hug?'

There would then proceed to be an incredibly awkward moment when he would have to approach this unknown lady and try to give a meaningful hug to a very large waistline that he couldn't even get his arms around. Meanwhile everyone in the room would be watching intensely. His face would be crushed against rolls of fat underneath a dress that had a very strange smell lingering on it. It would always be excruciatingly embarrassing as everyone would be watching and time seemed to stand still mid hug. It would be finished with a slobbery kiss planted on his forehead.

Jess interrupted this horrendous memory with a simple statement that brought panic to Finn and ruined his treasure finding plans in an instant.

'Well, my mum has had to go away for a few days and so I'm going to be staying here. And you're going to look after me.' With this bombshell she left his bedroom.

Finn couldn't believe it. He fell back onto his bed and put his hands on his face. Why now? Why did Jess have to come and stay now? It just wasn't fair.

There was no way he could tell her about the treasure map. It was only meant to be him and Rocket who knew. Finn could feel the book digging into his back from under the duvet. He had better get up and act as normal as possible otherwise his mum might tell something was up. Gosh, he still felt tired from the night's adventures.'

Just before Finn went downstairs, he made sure he changed the hiding place of the book (he had visions of Jess trying to look under his pillow or duvet to find it when he wasn't there.) Finn removed the dodgy bit of floorboard under his rug and stored the book in the secret place where he sometimes kept sweets and anything unusual that he thought could be long lost treasure.

Jess was sitting at the kitchen table eating a big sandwich. His mother was at the sink and looking out in the bright sunshine of the farmyard.

'Oh, hello there sleepy head' said his mum. 'You haven't slept that long for ages; you must have been tired?' Do you fancy some breakfast or should I say lunch!' His mum gave a chuckle and turned to see a still very sleepy Finn take his seat at the table.

'You're wearing the same clothes as yesterday Finny, don't you want to change?'

'That's what he was wearing in bed too Auntie Laura', said Jess with a knowing self-satisfied look at Finn.

He knew Jess was annoyed with him for not telling her what the black book was. This was going to be tricky.

'What's that dear? Did you really wear your shorts and t-shirt to bed? Why on earth did you do that? said Finn's mum as she splashed bubbles over the side of the sink with her washing up.

'Oh, I was just really tired last night and must have fallen asleep on my bed before changing,' said Finn, with the feeling that his cheeks were going ever so slightly red. He was rubbish at lying and knew anyone could see straight through him if he tried to tell a fib.

Jess stopped munching and continued to stare at him as if he was some strange exhibit in an exhibition. Finn could see her trying to work out what he had been up to, as she knew he was hiding something. The sandwich she was holding in her hands was half eaten and a juicy tomato was slowly dropping out towards the plate along with some lettuce and mayonnaise.

Finn returned Jess's stare and flicked his eyes down to warn her of the sandwich catastrophe that was about to take place without her knowing. Jess just managed to save the sandwich crisis in time and gave him an appreciative grin and nod of the head. Finn smiled and contained a laugh. Phew, at least he had a good reason for going redder now.

Jess was Finn's cousin. Her mum and Finn's mum were sisters. Jess had blond hair in a shoulder length bob. She had bright sparkly eyes and 'Cheeky cheeks' as Finn's mum would say. She loved to wear multi coloured socks with her trainers and she always wore dungarees. Finn had lost count of the times they had ended up covered in mud from messing around on the farm, only to be told off by his mum as they traipsed into the kitchen leaving a trail of slimy muck behind them.

Jess lived about an hour away near a big town. It wasn't a very nice area to be as it seemed so crowded with houses and there were no fields or woods. Finn hated going to stay there as he always had to sleep on a camp bed that was really uncomfortable. Once he had offered to camp outside in his tent with Jess for company but the main road backed onto their garden and the noise of the traffic kept him up all night. Typically, Jess had slept right through the night as she seemed used to the noise of the cars and lorries. Jess had two older brothers, but they had moved out a long time ago. That would explain why she was so used to getting her own way as her mum, Finn's Auntie Kate would spoil her rotten. Finn and Jess were in the same year but went to different schools.

They shared lots together and Jess was always round at the farm. Finn knew Jess would love to stay all the time. She didn't have a dad and it was a subject no one really spoke about. He had only talked about it with her once and she said she didn't know anything. Finn did like Jess and most of the time they got on, but occasionally she would get really girly and not want to be a part of his games and adventures.

'What are you two going to get up to today then? It's a lovely day out there again,' said Finn's mum.

'You could go and see if your Dad needs any help with the cows Finn?' This was one of those moments when

Finn realised it was more a statement than a suggestion. His mum gave him one of her looks which said all she needed to as she folded a tea towel.

'Yes mum, of course, I'll, I mean, we'll go and see Dad and offer him some help' said Finn. Jess's eyes lit up as he knew how much she loved helping on the farm. Do you know where he'll be?'

'Not sure, but I think he said he was going to be up on the top fields this afternoon. Whatever you get up to, don't be late for dinner though and remind your father as well.' With that, his mum bustled out of the kitchen to leave Finn and Jess looking at each other.

'Do you want another sandwich?, said Finn. 'I can help you make it this time, so it doesn't fall apart if you'd like?!'

'Thanks for that, but no, I'm okay actually. You just be thankful that I didn't start talking about old black books' responded Jess with her head wiggling from side to side just to annoy Finn even more.

These were the kind of situations when he and Jess fell out. She could be so stubborn sometimes. Finn had hoped she had forgotten about the secret book but, clearly, she still wanted to know more. It was going to be impossible for Finn not to tell her what it was.

Thinking about it, perhaps telling someone might be a good thing. It meant he didn't have to face it all on his own and if Jess was going to be staying for the next few days or so, maybe, they could go and look for the treasure together. It would definitely help to have another person's opinion on things. Would Jess be up for it? It was going to be risky and Finn well understood how scary it might be, just like when he went to Buckland Farm. Would Jess want to put herself in a place that was really scary?

It was Finn's turn to stare at Jess now as he thought through all the different options.

'Why are you looking at me so weirdly Finn?' said Jess uncomfortably.

'You're considering whether to tell me what that books all about aren't you?' Jess said smugly.

Finn remained silent but was inwardly very impressed that she could work out what he was thinking just by looking at him. Then he got it. He worked out how to tell if it was a good idea to tell Jess.

'Rocket, Rocky, where are you? Come here.' said Finn and he heard Rocket lurch up from her basket and pad her way over to his outstretched hand. Even though it was cold and wet, Finn loved nothing more than feeling Rocket nuzzle into his hand. Rocket was going to decide whether he told Jess or not.

Chapter 6. Rocket decides

Finn whispered his plan into Rockets ear. Rocket listened as any good dog does and gave a wag of her tail to acknowledge she clearly understood every word.

'There, so I've told Rocket and she can decide whether you should be told what that black book is about,' said Finn sitting back in his chair and crossing his arms.

'What do you mean?' said Jess.

'Well, Rocket was with me when I found the book and so she is part of the team, if she thinks you should know, then she'll walk around to you on your side of the table. If she stays on this side, then I'm sorry but she has decided that you can't be part of it.'

'That's ridiculous, but okay' said Jess. 'We know Rocket loves me just as much as you, why wouldn't she want me to know?'

They both sat in silence staring at each other. No one moved, not even Rocket. Their eyes were locked together with no blinking and dead pan faces.

Nothing happened for what seemed like ages and then from beneath the table there came the pad, pad, pad as Rocket made her way around to where Jess was sitting.

Jess's face slowly began to grow the faintest of smiles as she realised what was happening.

Rocket eventually made her way around the table and sat on her haunches next to Jess's chair.

The staring contest was broken with a triumphant cheer from Jess who reached down to hug and pat Rocket furiously.

'Ah, that's my good girl Rocky, good girl. You know you wanted me to know what nasty Finlay is keeping a secret.' At the word Finlay, Jess stared at Finn and her eyes widened even more.

Finn didn't know what else to do but stick his tongue out at her. It was clearly the reaction of a young child, but boy, did it feel good. He even followed it through by blowing a huge raspberry and that felt even better. It didn't last long though as Finn soon started laughing and so did Jess. They both broke out into such big belly laughs that even Rocket wanted to join in and gave a few barks. Tears were streaming down their cheeks and their sides hurt. And in that moment Finn realised that laughing like that is one of the best feelings in the whole world.

When they had calmed down and the contagious laughter had cancelled itself out to chuckles. Finn stood up to clear the plates away.

'I'm sorry Finn, I won't call you Finlay again. Only if I'm in real trouble and I need your help' said Jess.

'I'd appreciate that, that's twice you've called me by my full name and I've only been awake about half an hour! Come on let's get this stuff cleared away and go and find Dad. I've got something very exciting to show you.'

Inside Finn was relieved that he didn't have to carry the burden of the treasure map all by himself anymore. Jess would be a good adventure partner. Despite her girly moments she was brave and could run and swim just as fast as him. Finn was also aware that telling Jess about the book was special for her as she didn't have a lot to look forward to at her home. It would explain why she wanted to be here all the time on the farm.

It was funny thought Finn. He hadn't even found the treasure yet, but already he had experienced things and found things out about himself that he didn't know he could do. His trip to Buckland Farm had tested him beyond anything he had ever done before but he had come through it. He realised he was learning to think about others more and what they might be feeling. It made him feel better inside. To put it simply, he wanted to be the person Rocket thought he was. He knew Rocket would go and stand next to Jess in the kitchen, but he realised how special it made her feel by that happening.

'So, let's see that book then,' Jess said as she skipped up the stairs two at time in excitement.

'Hang on a minute, I must go and brush my teeth! My mum is always reminding me to do it and she has a cunning way of knowing if I haven't,' said Finn has he swung around the bannister towards the bathroom.

'Brush your teeth? That's a bit weird?! We've just had lunch. Who brushes their teeth after lunch?'

Finn didn't want Jess to see his secret hiding place under the rug in his room. He thought that if he could get her in the bathroom for long enough, he could quickly get back to his room to remove the book and put it back under his pillow without her seeing where he got it from.

'Where's your toothbrush anyway?' said Finn as he stood in front of the mirror.

Whenever, Jess stayed she always slept in the spare room halfway down the corridor. Finn knew that her bag wouldn't be unpacked yet and would probably still be sat on her bed with her toothbrush inside it.

'Okay, I'll get it. But I'm not going to make a habit of brushing my teeth after lunch everyday' said Jess as she went into her room.

Finn could hear her rummaging around in her bag and smiled at himself in the bathroom mirror.

He started to brush his teeth frantically as Jess walked in with her toothbrush. Finn spat into the sink and shoved the tooth paste at her as he dashed out of the room. He scooted back down the landing and slid the rug off the loose floorboard in his room. He grabbed the black book, placed the floor back together and shoved the rug back with his foot as he stood up just as Jess emerged from the bathroom, with white toothpaste marks at the corner of her mouth making it look like she had been eating an ice-cream.

'Well, that's the first and the last time I'm going to clean my teeth after lunch,' said Jess as she wiped away the tooth paste marks from her mouth with the back of her hand.

'What is it then that you want to show me? It's that book. What's so special about it? And where did you get it?' she said pointing at it.

As Jess spoke, Finn placed the book on the bed and slowly opened it to reveal the hidden compartment inside. It seemed to feel as special as the first time he opened it. Both children stared at the yellowish folded piece of paper in the secret place and they both looked at each other drawing in breath.

Finn then reached in and took the paper. He started to unfold it just as he had done in the twinkling moonlight. With all the commotion of Jess arriving, he hadn't really had time to think about the map or the strange vehicle driving down to Buckland Farm in the dead of night. Could it have been Farmer Cramner behind the wheel? What would he have been doing going down there at that time?

Jess's mouth hung open in pure amazement as Finn finished unfolding the paper. The sunlight shone brightly through the window making it difficult to see the map. Finn moved slightly into shadow from the curtain so they could both see it better.

'Wow....what is it?' said Jess in a whisper, her eyes shining wide with wonder.

'It's a treasure map, look here at the cross that's marked.'

Finn held the map for Jess to see clearly. Both sets of eyes soaked up all they could see on the piece of paper.

'So, that's the castle with the cross marked,' said Jess. 'But what are the other things drawn in the woods around it? Look, I think that is a waterfall,' she pointed to another symbol that looked like water hitting rocks. How about this one, it's a funny shape, and why is it coloured in? Jess was pointing to a dark circle about a finger's width from the castle. There was a dotted line from the dark circle to the castle.

'I don't know,' Finn said. 'It looks like it could be a tunnel.'

'I can't believe you have this, where on earth did you get it?'

Finn was half listening to Jess but his attention was on the writing at the bottom of the map that he couldn't read in the dark the first time he had seen it. The letters were swirly and difficult to read.

Beware of the treasure. Beware of who guards the treasure. Beware to use the treasure wisely or the same fate awaits you.

Finn read the words slowly and then read them again with his hands ever so slightly shaking. He could feel the hairs on the back of his neck stand on end and he took a big gulp when he had finished. Jess continued to stare and then met his gaze with an equally puzzled look.

'What does it mean Finn? Beware who guards the treasure? What treasure? Please tell me, tell me everything.'

'You had better sit down.'

With that, Jess and Finn sat on the bed as Finn explained all that had happened since he found the balloon in the hedge yesterday afternoon. He told her of the note, his midnight trip to Buckland

Farm and of the strange vehicle he had seen as he was leaving. As he spoke, they both just stared at the map in his hands.

Having Jess know, now made it even more real. Finn could see from her reactions that she was just as excited as he was. Could Jess also tell how nervous he was as well? The writing at the bottom of the map had changed everything again. It was all very well looking for some supposed treasure in a wood but now it seemed way more serious with a warning that it was guarded by someone or something? And what did it mean when it said use the treasure wisely or the same fate awaits you?

Finn didn't really understand what the word fate meant but he knew it probably wasn't good as it was used as warning.

Chapter 7. Not Famer Cramner again?

Jess hadn't said much since Finn had finished telling her why it was, they were sitting on his bed holding a treasure map. She turned to look at him and took hold of his hand and squeezed it.

'Finn, this is the most exciting thing that has ever happened to us! We must go and find the treasure.'

'Yes, I know,' said Finn, 'but what about what it says at the bottom of the map?'

'Oh, that's just put there to scare people, I'm sure they used to write lots of that kind of thing in the old days, Come on, let's go now and find the castle in the woods,' said Jess, jumping off the bed and dragging Finn up.

'Hang on,' said Finn, 'It's not that simple, we can't just go walking up into those woods.

We don't even know where we are going, and those woods are massive.'

'That's why we've got a map....deerrr brain,' said Jess.

'I know what the maps for, but I don't even know if we are allowed in those woods. I have never been in them. What if we get lost, then we'll be in real trouble!'

'That's what an adventure is all about,' sighed Jess in an exasperated voice. 'You know how we have been looking forward to a proper adventure for ages. This is it! We don't have to pretend anymore. That map says there's treasure to be found. This is amazing. Come on, let's just go and see the woods. We don't have to go into them. We can just have a look from the top of the fields. We need to go and help your dad anyway. You're the one who said that.'

Jess tugged at his sleeve and tried to pull him out of the room. Finn didn't know why he was suddenly having a change of heart about it all. Jess hadn't experienced what he had gone through at Buckland Farm and how scared he was. What would happen to her if she got scared? Would she just run off in the woods and leave him? Then they would both would be lost, and it would be really scary. She also didn't seem to fear the warnings at the bottom of the map.

Finn didn't want to seem afraid in front of her but for some reason he just couldn't get the feeling out from the back of his mind that they were both about to enter an adventure way beyond what they had imagined.

Together, they wandered up the farm track into the fields. The map was safely tucked into his pocket. Insects buzzed around them and they could see grasshoppers jumping at random across the path. Rocket bobbed along beside them, happy to be out in the open again. Every so often she would look up to see if Jess was looking at her. A kestrel hoovered in the warm afternoon sunshine waiting for its prey to show themselves.

'You know Jess, we won't necessarily be able to go and find the castle today. It's already the afternoon and you heard what my mum said about being late for dinner. We need time to explore those woods and the last thing we want to do is get lost in there as it's getting dark,' said Finn trying to sound very responsible.

Jess agreed with a nod of her head and then stopped, turning towards him.

'Look Finn, you're in charge. I wouldn't know where to start looking. It's your map. I'm just happy that you shared it with me. I'm sorry if I was too pushy about the book. I was just interested. I do find this really exciting though.'

Jess looked up towards the woods and carried on with what she was thinking.

'It does look scary up there even in the daytime. It's seems so dark and mysterious. There's a reason we have never been exploring in there before now.'

'I know, it's because we have never found the guts to go in there!' said Finn with a half-hearted smile.

'We should go first thing tomorrow morning that will give us a good amount of time to explore. Perhaps we could take a picnic with us. We don't need to tell your mum or dad where we are going...We could say we're going fishing down at the river for the day,' said Jess quickly as the idea formed in her mind and she rushed to get it out.

'Yes, let's wait until tomorrow,' Finn said, relieved. He felt much more at peace about not going in the woods right there and then. He had already had enough frights that day.

'Look, there's your dad, up there in the corner of the field. Is he talking to someone?' Jess pointed to where she was looking. She was right. Finn's father was talking to someone. Whoever it was wasn't standing in the field, they were just inside the wood. Finn had a sinking feeling who it could be.

They started walking faster up the track to get a clearer view. With each step they made, Finn could see more of Farmer Cramner chatting to his father. He was standing in almost exactly the same spot as yesterday when he had shouted at Finn. He was wearing the same scruffy clothes and Finn was now doubly sure it was him in the Land Rover in the middle of the night at Buckland Farm. But why was he there?

Jess had run a few yards ahead of him to catch up with Rocket as they made their way to the top of the field.

'Hello there Jessie,' said Finn's dad as he gave her a squeeze. 'I heard you were coming to stay for a few days. You looking after Rocky then?'

Jess didn't seem bothered that she had broken up the conversation between her uncle and this rather strange looking man with a hairy fat belly hanging over his trousers. Farmer Cramner stood there leaning on a stick at the edge of the woods watching the conversation whilst chewing a piece of grass. His belly looked even uglier than yesterday and even Jess noticed there was a very strong smell coming from his direction. He had a permanent scowl etched on his lips.

Finn caught up to them and did his best not to look at Farmer Cramner who was studying him intensely.

'Hi Dad, we thought we'd find you up here. Mum said you might need a hand?' said Finn hesitantly.

Finn's father ruffled his hair with his huge farmer hands and patted him on the back in a proud father-like way. Finn could see the slight look of sadness on Jess's face as she witnessed this.

'Well Finny, I was just having a chat with our neighbour here, Mr Cramner. He says that some people have been intruding on his land and going in his woods? You haven't seen anyone around here doing that now have you?' said Finn's father giving him a very gentle squeeze on the shoulder.

'If you see anyone youngster, you tell your pa.' said Farmer Cramner in a menacing way. Was this his way of getting Finn back for yesterday, or did he even know that Finn had been to Buckland Farm? He wasn't seen in the grass, was he? Farmer Cramner gave Finn such a horrible grimace that Finn had to look away.

'You mark my words, anyone caught in these woods will live to regret it. I'll 'ave my dogs on them if I see or hear anyone on my land.' With that Farmer Cramner touched his hat to Finn's father and made to turn around. However, his large belly and inability to move anywhere fast made it very difficult to turn his body. It reminded Finn of a hippo. With a great amount of difficulty and some very strange noises, he eventually managed to hobble away back into the dark depths of the woods.

Finn immediately looked at Jess, whose face, and shoulders drooped. She was thinking exactly the same as him. Things had just got a lot more complicated. As if going into the woods wasn't hard enough, now Farmer Cramner was on the lookout even more and he had spoken with his dad about it. And Farmer Cramner said he had dogs he was going to let loose on people.

Finn's Father watched Cramner retreat into the undergrowth and pursed his lips together at the same time as giving a squint, which made it obvious that he was thinking hard.

'Watch out for him you two,' he warned them. 'You just don't know how he is going to react sometimes. A very strange fellow. Always has been.'

'What was he talking to you about dad' asked Finn.

'Oh, I haven't seen him in a few months, we were just talking about the cows and his farm. He was snooping around the edge of the woods here and I started talking to him.'

'Why was he here? Was he looking for something?' asked Finn. Had Cramner any idea about the note on the balloon? It all seemed so strange that he was in the same spot yesterday as well as going to Buckland Farm.

'Don't know,' said Finn's father as he went to rub Rocket's ears. 'Anyway, we should be getting back. Mum will want a hand with dinner. Could you do me a favour and help walk the cows in? You'd better keep Rocky close; I don't want her scaring any of our ladies.'

Finn took one last look into the woods and wondered how far in they would have to go to find the castle. It can't be a normal castle now; it must be in ruins. This made it even more mysterious. He was sure that he would have heard his parents talk about a castle if it was still a proper castle like the ones you see in films or in books. He couldn't resist asking his dad a few more questions.

'Dad, is there a castle in those woods? And does Mr Cramner own them?'

Jess shot him a furious look as if to say what on earth was he doing asking such obvious questions.

Finn shrugged a response with his shoulders back to her so that his dad didn't see.

Finn's father stopped and looked down at him. Along with his mum, he was able to give him one of those stares that said so many things. Finn began to feel himself squirming under the intense gaze.

'Now, why would you be asking such things Finn?' said his father.

'Oh, I was just wondering. We, er, have a project at school next term on castles and I wondered....er.... what..... What the closest castle was to our farm,' Finn knew this sounded pathetic and he could see Jess roll her eyes in her head.

Finn's father continued to hold his gaze and Finn knew his dad would already be well on the way to working out why he asked those questions.

If only he hadn't been so stupid and thought before he spoke. His dad could stop them going anywhere which would ruin their whole adventure. Jess knew this and by her body language had already resigned herself to the fact that Finn's father was about to tell them not to go anywhere near the woods and they would be in big trouble if they did.

Before Finn could dig himself any deeper into the hole he had created, his father spoke.

'I have heard old stories of a castle, but I have never seen it myself. I've lived on this farm all my life, but I've only been in those woods a few times when I was younger. Yes, they belong to Mr Cramner. You just be careful Finn and Jess, as I said before, he's a very strange fellow.' He paused as if wondering to say the next thing. 'One thing I found odd though, when he spoke to us. He said that he would set his dogs loose if anyone was on his land. I didn't think he had any dogs.' With that he gave a wink to Finn and walked off calling to the cows.

Finn stood there and couldn't believe what he had just heard or seen. His dad had definitely winked at him. What did that mean? Was that his dad's way of saying he could go and try to discover the castle? He never said that they couldn't go into the woods, did he?

Jess looked puzzled and came closer to Finn holding Rocket by her collar.

'You are such a plonker sometimes Finn! You couldn't have made it any more obvious about us wanting to go and explore in those woods. Why didn't you just tell your dad about the treasure map? You muppet. Still, I wasn't expecting your dad to say what he did,' said Jess.

'I know, he never said we couldn't go. He just said be careful of Mr Cramner. Did you see him wink at me when he said about the dogs?'

In that brief moment, Finn felt like something unspoken had passed between him and his dad. He smiled to himself as he turned to walk down to the farm. The cows were tramping their way down to the milking sheds. He loved walking them down. They always seemed to go at one speed, their heads lolling from side to side, each of them following the one in front. It was a view he had seen countless times, but it never became boring. It always gave him time to think. The only thing going round his head now was what the castle could look like. How intact would it be? Would there be staircases and rooms they could explore. Would there be a dungeon? Every castle had to have a dungeon didn't it?

Chapter 8. A slightly awkward dinner

By the time they got back to the farm after helping with the milking, Finn's mum had made a wonderful dinner for them all. Roast chicken with all the trimmings was spread out on the large table in the kitchen. The steam from the food hung in the air and the amazing smells made Finn and Jess's mouths' water as they washed their hands in the sink.

'The towel for drying is just on the back of the chair, there dear.'

'Thanks Auntie Laura, this looks awesome,' said Jess as she finished drying and threw the towel at Finn so it landed on his head.

Finn's mother was pleased to see them all together when they came in. She had made a special effort to cook this roast for Jess, mainly as she knew how much Jess loved being part of the family. For years now, she had tried to persuade her sister, Jess's mum, to come and live with them in one of the farm cottages. It made so much sense; Jess could go to the same school as Finn and they would have each other to play within the holidays. There was a cottage sat empty that would be perfect for them.

After they sat down, Finn's father started to say Grace. Jess had her hands together and respectfully bowed her head. Sometimes she couldn't always hear exactly what her uncle was saying as he prayed but she knew to say Amen at the end and not move too quickly straight away as it would be obvious she hadn't been listening. This Grace however, Jess couldn't help looking up through her eyebrows to see if Finn was doing what he was meant to. Through the steam from the vegetables their eyes met and they gave each other an excited smile. Jess couldn't get the thought of the treasure map out of her head. She was so excited by it. It felt a bit like Christmas Eve when you have that bubbly, fuzzy feeling all day long as you know the next day is Christmas. How was she going to get to sleep tonight?

They all tucked into their roast dinners and there was a hungry silence. Finn's dad sat at the head of the table and seemed to have a mountain of food on his plate.

'So, what are you two going to get up to tomorrow?' said Auntie Laura chopping into a roast potato.

Finn and Jess looked at each other and at the very same time they both exclaimed in a rush.

'*We're going to go fishing and take a picnic.*'

As soon as they had spoken, they knew that it sounded made up. There was an awkward silence as Finn's mother and father looked at each other suspiciously.

'Well, if that's okay Mum?' said Finn trying to claw some normality back into the conversation.

Jess had her eyes firmly fixed on her plate. Finn could see that she was going red with embarrassment. He understood why, it was one thing for him to tell his mum and dad a porky, but for Jess to lie to her auntie and uncle, that felt more wrong in a way.

'Well, you'd better take your raincoats and it's going to be a bit of a soggy picnic. It's forecast to storm tomorrow and it's going to rain all day.' said Finn's dad as he loaded another massive helping up on his fork.

'Really?' said Finn, trying not to sound too disappointed. Inside he was gutted. There was no way they could go up into the woods now. Not in a storm with constant rain. They needed to go in the dry. They would have to wait. Finn looked at Jess again who had taken the news just as badly as him. She gave him a small shrug and sandwiched her lips together whilst raising her eyebrows.

'Don't worry about that love, there's lots to do inside,' said Finn's mum reassuringly. 'You could build a den in the attic or finish that large puzzle you started?'

'Hmmm,' said Finn unenthusiastically. Jess and he would be stuck inside all day tomorrow. He was not good at being kept indoors. He always preferred to be outside.

The rest of dinner seemed to pass Finn and Jess by in a fog of disappointment. It was like someone had cancelled Christmas with only a few hours to go.

Finn's parents chatted about what it was like when they were growing up and how they 'had to make the best of things, even when the weather was bad'.

Finn was realising it was becoming increasingly easy to switch off to what his parents were saying when they talked about the 'good old days' or if the phrase 'when I was young' came into a sentence; it was the cue for him to drift off into his own thoughts.

Jess looked just as uninterested as him from what he could tell. Her glum face was only broken when she remembered she was guest at the table. Every so often she felt it was important to nod her head in agreement if her auntie or uncle said something.

'Finn....Finny, what do you think love?' asked his mum bringing Finn back to the present. He had absolutely no idea what had just been said to him as he had been about to enter a castle through the gate house in his imagination. He had completely missed the last bit of their conversation.

'Yes, I think it's a great idea,' said Finn, hoping this was the right response.

Jess gave a suppressed chuckle and his parents both smiled.

'What, what did I say that was so funny?'

'You just agreed that you think it's a great idea that you to go to bed right now! You don't normally want to go to bed this early but you were tired this morning and you do look tired now dear.' Finn's mum said with a smile.

'Oh, did I, do I?' said Finn, resigned to that fact that he was obviously looking very tired. His mum's roast had given him that sleepy feeling that often comes on after a big meal.

'Well, I'll head upstairs then. Do you want a hand with the washing up Mum?'

'No, thank you for offering. Jess and your father can help me with clearing up. You head up to bed sleepy head. Sleep well.' Finn's mum gave him a kiss on the forehead and a gentle squeeze as he made his way past her.

'Night Dad, night Jess.'

'Don't forget to put your pyjamas on this time!' said Jess as Finn started up the stairs.

'Night Finny,' called his dad from the kitchen as he reached the landing.

'I'll come and tuck you in when I've helped Mum with the washing up. Sleep well.'

Finn was in a sleepy stupor by now. He couldn't wait to crash into bed. He hadn't felt this tired in ages. Just before he got into bed he remembered he still had the treasure map in the pocket of his shorts from earlier. He carefully placed the folded map back in the old book which was still under his pillow. He then shut his eyes and drifted off to sleep almost immediately. He didn't even stir when his mum and dad came up to kiss him goodnight.

Chapter 9. Questions from the attic

The first thing Finn could hear when he awoke was the rain hammering against his bedroom window. It sounded as if hundreds of tiny nails were being thrown against the panes. He turned over in the snugness of his warm duvet and listened. There is something very special about being all cosy in bed and listening to a storm rage outside. It was one of life's free presents. Finn knew it was definitely wet rain that he could hear. Sometimes it would rain, he thought, and the rain didn't get him as wet as it should have. He could be outside for ages and not really feel very damp at all. Finn called that dry rain. Wet rain was the type of rain that got you soaked through in seconds. It didn't matter what you were wearing, you just got wet. It would come down as if rivers were being turned on from the sky.

After a while, Finn leant up on his elbows to peer through the soaked windowpanes down to the flooded farmyard below. Whenever it rained like this, there would always be an area in the corner of the yard that made a mini lake as the drain got blocked and overflowed.

Finn remembered how he and Jess, had once put their wellies and coats on and gone out to play in a storm similar to this one. They had got absolutely drenched through, but didn't care as they ran through the puddles and made a point of sitting down in the farmyard mini lake. The water came up to their waists! Finn's mum had made them take all their clothes off outside in the yard apart from their underwear. They then sat shivering on stools, wrapped in large warm towels in front of the open fire in the kitchen, sipping hot chocolate.

He wasn't in the mood to do that today. Finn reached under his pillow and pulled out the black book. He sat up in bed and studied the folded treasure map. Where did this come from? What were these strange symbols down the sides? He had looked at it so many times now, but he was still none the wiser. It seemed each time he saw it, there would be another question in his head that he didn't know the answer to.

Down the corridor, he heard the familiar creak of the floorboards as Jess shuffled her sleepy walk to the bathroom. He remembered his mum's idea from last night's dinner about building a den in the attic. He had always loved doing that. Finn knew just where to wedge the rugs into the roof beams so they would stay. He could create all kinds of tunnels and secret rooms given enough blankets and old boxes.

At breakfast, Jess and he agreed that building a den was probably the most fun they could have that day. They did think about going outside, but after staring out of the window for only a few seconds they settled on staying dry in the attic instead.

'Mum, are you okay if me and Jess go and build a den in the attic?'

'Of course dear, do you want some snacks to take up with you? I've got some muffins in a tin from last week.' Without waiting for an answer as, his mum reached up for the tin that was on top of the fridge.

'Do you want a hand Auntie Laura?' offered Jess.

'No, I'm okay thanks Jessie, you go on and head upstairs. I'll bring up a plate of goodies with a drink in a bit.'

'Thanks Mum,' said Finn as he and Jess bounded upstairs in excitement. Auntie Laura bustled around the kitchen chatting to Rocket who was lying down in her basket with her tail wagging over the side.

'Poor Rocky, it's miserable out there today. No going out running in the fields for you. Still, the storm is meant to blow itself out by this afternoon. I'm sure Finn and Jess will take you out for walk when it dries up.' Rocket gave a doggy harrumph and closed her eyes. Time for her to go chasing rabbits in her sleep.

Up in the attic, Finn and Jess were working hard on making their den the best one they had ever made. They could hear the rain pounding the tiles just above their heads. Jess had named the den 'Jess's Princess Palace' which Finn had turned his nose up at as he could smell the faint whiff of girl floating into the situation. Finn wanted to call it 'Fort Finn', a far better choice he reckoned. They had discussed about asking Finn's Mum to decide between the two names, but then they realised that she wouldn't want to choose a winner.

Finn could hear his mum say something along the lines of,

'Ah, they are both lovely names you two and do you know, I can't choose between them. Why don't you call it Jess and Finn's Palace's Fort?'

This would be most unsatisfactory as a clear winner had to be the priority. As was always the case in any kind of competition being judged by parents, they could never choose an outright winner.

Finn and Jess were very proud of what they had created. It had three entrances and two main chambers which could be reached by secret tunnels. Blankets and old duvets were hung over chairs and boxes to create a magical patch work of colour and levels. In some places the duvets had dipped down over the tunnels making it very difficult to climb along. Finn busied himself by going around fixing any loose blankets and filling up any holes he found with pillows.

The attic was a place that Finn didn't go into very often. It had that funny smell that only attics seemed have; a mixture of dust and musty old things. It was only on rainy days like these or when he was asked to get the Christmas decorations down that he climbed up the rickety ladder. It was full of junk from years back. He has never seen half the stuff in there as the light didn't work at the far end and he was too scared to go down there by himself.

'There, I think we are nearly finished,' Finn said as he stuffed one last flowery cushion into a hole. It was very important not to have any holes in a den. He stepped back carefully to have a look at their construction. The den had done a great job of taking their minds off the fact they couldn't be up in the woods exploring.

'It looks just like a Princess Palace,' said Jess coming to stand next to him with her arms crossed, knowing that it would start the semi argument again.

'Fort,' said Finn straightaway.

'Palace,' replied Jess in an extravagantly royal manner, as if she were a Princess herself.

Finn gave her a smirk and lost the will to keep the contest going when he saw that Jess had a rather large cobweb hanging in her hair. She must have got it on her when she was squirming around in the corner he thought. This was a bit of a problem because, alongside mushrooms and snails, there was nothing that Jess hated more than spiders. He knew what reaction she would have if he was to tell her and it wouldn't be good. The last time Jess had come near a spider was in the bathroom when one had crawled out of a plug hole and Finn thought he had gone deaf in his left ear, she screamed so loud.

He wasn't sure what to do as he really didn't want her to freak out and the fact they were up in the attic made it worse because Jess would try and run around, and no doubt wipe herself out on something, or worse still, damage the den.

He thought about trying to wipe it off her without her realising what he was doing but he knew that just wouldn't work. The more he looked at the stringy dusty cobweb clinging to the side of her head, the more he knew that Jess would go completely mad. He had to think of something.

'Hey, Jess, let's go down this end of the attic. I haven't been down this end in ages.' Finn grabbed her arm and led her along the narrow planks between the beams. He didn't want to admit he hadn't been down there at all, as he was too scared normally.

'It's a lot darker down this end,' said Jess, a little unsure as to why Finn has suddenly grabbed her arm. She thought she was just about to win the battle of what the den was going to be called.

Because they had spent so long up there building the den, their eyes had got used to the light and adjusted so they could see more than normal. The other end of the attic was even dustier and smelt worse. It had all kinds of boxes and crates stacked up. There were old umbrellas, wooden tennis rackets, rolled up posters and bed headboards; empty picture frames; hat stands; garden tools and an old dirty traffic cone. It was as if Finn's mum and dad had gone to the local antiques shop and brought everything they didn't want and shoved it up in the attic.

'Hey, look at this,' Jess said as she started rummaging around in an old box. 'These gloves are amazing!'

Jess had found a very old elegant pair of white silk gloves and was trying them on. 'I bet they were owned by a Princess once when she lived in palace just like our den!' Finn noticed the slight dig and did think about mentioning the cobweb on the side of her head but thought he would keep that in the bag in case he needed to use it later.

It was amazing to look at all the different objects collected and stored in his attic. How weird that they have been here for years, Finn thought. He realised that at the time they would have been the newest thing to own and probably cost a lot of money. Now they were just useless, dusty boxes full of things that people didn't want or need anymore.

'What's this?' said Jess as she pulled a book out of the bottom of a chest. The large book was a deep red colour with intricate gold swirls printed around the edge. It was about the size of a big encyclopaedia and looked like it weighed a fair bit by the way Jess was struggling to pick it up.

She blew the top layer of dust off and scraped her forearm over the front cover to see if there was a title on it.

'Finn, this looks really old and mysterious.'

Finn could see what Jess meant straight away. He helped her hold the book as she attempted to open it. It gave off a smell of musty pipe smoke. Finn's grandpa has smoked a pipe; he was reminded of when he was younger, when he would sit on the floor stroking Rocket while his grandpa told him stories of when he was a boy and life on the farm. The pipe smoke would hang in the air around his Grandpa as if he was a volcano that had just erupted.

'Let's take this book into the light where we can get a better look at it,' said Jess. It took both of them to carry the book along the planks back towards the entrance to the ladder where it was lighter. The excitement of the den had been replaced by their new discovery. It didn't look quite as magnificent as it had done before they ventured to the other end of the attic.

Finn placed the book down and gave a quick sideways glance to Jess. He could hear his mother coming up the stairs with what would hopefully be some of her homemade muffins and a drink.

Before his mother got to the top of the stairs, Finn opened the book and his mouth dropped in amazement.

'Finn, Jess, I've got your snack. Those stairs seemed a lot steeper carrying all this up here,' echoed Finn's mum in a slightly out of breath way from down on the landing.

'Finn, Jess, can you hear me?...Jess, Finn....Hello up there?'

Finn and Jess were in a trance. They were both staring wide eyed at the open page of the book in front of them. They couldn't speak.

'Finn, for goodness sake, can you hear me? Are you alright, Jess?'

'Hi Mum, thanks for that, yes, we're fine,' replied Finn in a rather rushed, completely distracted way. He was totally absorbed by what was in front of him on the page.

'Oh, good to hear that you two are still alive, please don't make too many crumbs with the muffins.' said his mum with a sigh, as she gently placed the tray on the floor at the bottom of the ladder.

Muffins were the last thing on Finn's and Jess's mind.

The page Finn had opened the book on, had a drawing of a castle. Not just any castle but the very same castle that was drawn on the treasure map.

'Oh, my goodness,' said Jess, putting her hand to her mouth in complete shock. 'That is the same...'

'Yes, I know,' said Finn, interrupting her before she could finish.

They both just stared at the page. The picture of the castle was more detailed than the one on the map. It showed knights in armour on horseback riding into the gate house; soldiers on the battlements; ladies in long colourful dresses with pointed hats; children playing with wooden shields and swords; servants carrying barrels of wine and bundles of wood; brightly coloured flags flew from the turrets. In those few seconds, it was as if the castle had come to life in front of their eyes. Below the picture, there was writing in the same swirly style as the note currently under Finn's pillow.

'What does it say?' Jess asked eagerly?

Finn squinted that little bit harder as he tried to make out the words.

The castle above was a Royal Fortress. It was built at the end of the twelfth century and became an important defensive position for the local Barons. The castle grew in popularity, many kings and queens visited during their reigns. King Richard I declared the woods around the castle to be a royal hunting ground. There are many legends attached to the castle and the surrounding area, the most famous relating to Baron Athelstan, who lived in at the castle in 1367. The legend says that the Baron tried to steal the castle's treasure during a large storm. He ran through the woods with the treasure in the dead of night and was never seen again. Over the years, there have been many accounts of local woodsmen hearing unearthly noises near where the castle ruins lie. There have even been some sightings of a strange beast living in the woods around the castle, but nothing was ever confirmed.

After Finn had finished reading the passage aloud, he turned to Jess.

'What does unearthly noises mean? The bit where the woodsmen had heard 'unearthly' noises?'

'I don't know,' said Jess in a half whisper as she continued to study the detail of the picture.

'I do like those dresses the ladies are wearing.'

Finn couldn't believe all Jess was thinking about were the dresses. What about the legend of the castle and how people had seen a strange beast in the woods? Not just any woods, the woods at the top of the field near his farm. Finn didn't know whether to be troubled by this news or not. It certainly made the adventure more exciting.

'Hang on, do you think that the strange beast that it talks about is the same thing that the map warns us about when it says, 'beware of who guards the treasure?' he said nervously.

Jess looked up and realised what he was saying. The air in the attic suddenly felt colder and she gave a shiver. Her mind began to paint pictures of what the beast could look like as it lived up in the woods all by itself.

'What's on the next page? Is there anything else about the castle?' she said trying to change the subject away from the uncomfortable thought of what might be living in the woods.

Finn turned the page. His heart stopped. The page that was meant to be there was gone. It had been ripped out. Except that it wasn't ripped out completely. There was still a bit of scraggy paper attached to the book. In a missed heartbeat, Finn knew that the treasure map he had found in Buckland Farm had been from this book. The writing was the same and he was sure that if he matched it up with the book it would fit.

Jess had worked this all out in the same moment and gave a small cry of alarm. Once again, her hand went to her mouth when she realised what they had discovered. A shiver ran up her spine, but this time it was not the cold. Nervous and excited energy flooded through her as she felt herself being sucked further into this mystery with each passing second.

Someone, somewhere, had torn the page out. But when? How long had this book been in the attic? How old was the book? So many questions fizzed around her mind, it was difficult to think clearly.

'Right,' said Finn. 'We have to go and look up in those woods. Who knows what we will find?' A steely determination had entered his voice. He had similar feelings to Jess about it all, but deep down he knew what they had to do to.

'Listen, I think the rains stopped,' Jess whispered as she looked up to the attic roof. The two of them had been so wrapped up in finding the book, they hadn't noticed the hammering on the tiles above them had ceased.

'If the storm has passed and it's clear, shall we go for a little explore up into the woods? We don't have to go far. It can be a practice for tomorrow? We can take Rocky with us to warn us of anything. She has the best hearing and will bark if we happen to come across any strange beast,' said Jess with a grin.

'Perhaps the strange beast is Farmer Cramner!' replied Finn as it suddenly came into his head. They both laughed at this and the tension was broken.

'Yes, let's go and see what the weather is doing. We shouldn't go too far but a little explore will be fun. We must be so careful not to get caught though.'

'What shall we do with this book?' said Finn. 'I think we should leave it up here. Let's put it in the den so it's out the way. No one else is going to be coming up here.'

Chapter 10. What's that noise?

The field was squelchy as they trudged up to where the woods began. Their welly boots made that fantastic sucking noise whenever they slurped out of a fresh puddle or patch of mud. The air smelt clean, as it always did after a summer storm. The cobweb in Jess's hair was blown away in a gust of wind. She had no idea it had gone and probably for the best Finn thought. He smiled to himself when he realised the expression his mum used actually came true. Their knees were tickled by the slimy wet grass, but Finn and Jess didn't care as they were outside again in the warm sunshine. Rocket was doing that crazy running thing that dogs sometimes do when they haven't had a chance to let off energy in a while. She charged around, changing direction and then galloped off at full speed again.

'Rocky, what are you up to, you crazy dog?' laughed Jess as Rocket hurtled towards them only to veer away at the last moment.

The shadows of the wood came closer and the reality of what they were about to do dawned on them. Finn had never been very far into the woods, ever. As he looked ahead of him, all he could see was a dark green blur of branches and tree trunks. Vague patches of light shone down at random intervals on the woodland floor. The darkness seemed almost too still. The cool, damp air wafted onto them as if they were being coated with a mysterious layer of dew, granting them permission to enter its depths.

Finn and Jess looked at each other. They didn't need to talk, the look of apprehension said it all. They knew what the other one would be thinking. Rocket gave a small whine. Finn looked around them and made sure no one was watching. His parents knew they had gone out, but they only thought, Finn and Jess were walking Rocket in the fields. There is no way they would have allowed them to go into the woods. Especially after what Finn's dad had said about Farmer Cramner.

There was no sign of anyone.

'Quick, let's go, come on,' Finn had had enough of waiting. He jumped up over the first bush and landed heavily using his hands to stop himself falling over. Wearing wellies and trying to move fast was not going to be easy. He could hear Jess land behind him with a grunt. The excited energy flowed through his body, it made him feel alive and alert like he had never experienced before. He crouched as he ran, keeping his body low, just in case anyone could see him from the fields. Jess caught up with him and they were already slightly out of breath. He couldn't believe where he was. He was in the place he had seen a thousand times, but he had never been brave enough to ever go this far into them. His heart was pounding as he ran further away from the safety of the warm field and further into the darkness of the cold wood.

Jess was loving every second. She was a good runner and even wearing wellies and dungarees didn't bother her. Rocket was by her side, springing around trees and ducking under branches as this was the easiest thing to do in the world.

Finn prayed that Farmer Cramner wasn't anywhere nearby. They weren't very good at being quiet. Their wellies didn't help but every step seemed to crunch and crack branches beneath their feet. Time to slow down a bit Finn thought. He crouched down at the bottom of a big old oak tree. They were both panting for breath but had an elated fuzzy feeling as they scoured the area they had run into. The field seemed a long way back now. Finn put his finger to his lips to show Jess they weren't to make any noise. Steadily he adjusted his position and looked around the tree to see if he could work out which way they should go. He hadn't brought the map with them deliberately. This was only meant to be a short mission into the woods.

Jess snuck up behind him and whispered into his ear.

'How far are we going to go? I don't think we should lose sight of the field. We could get lost otherwise?'

'Don't worry, I have a plan' said Finn, delving into this shorts pocket. 'I have brought an old piece of paper to help us.'

'Oh, that's great,' said Jess in a sarcastic way. 'A piece of paper, that's just what we need!'

'No stupid, you don't understand. I am going to rip a small bit off every so often and it lies on the floor. We can then retrace our steps and find the bits of paper that will lead us back to the field.' Finn said very proudly. 'I saw this technique used in an army book once, except they used flour instead, but I thought it would be too tricky to get flour, so I got a piece of paper instead.'

Judging by the funny face she pulled along with a slight frown, Finn could see that Jess wasn't as impressed with his idea as he was.

'What happens when the paper blows away or gets eaten by a small animal? What happens if we can't find the piece of paper because it is too small? Oh Finn, you get full marks for the idea but zero for actually how this is going to work in real life.' Jess said in a harsh whisper. 'Look we can't go too far now anyway. Let's see if we can find a path, follow me.'

Jess moved off in front of Finn and for the second time in a relatively short space of time, he found himself sticking his tongue out at her as she moved off through the undergrowth. He felt a little annoyed that she hadn't liked his idea of the paper trail back to the field. Still, he was going to do it anyway and so he carefully tore a small corner off and dropped it on the floor. He was more fed up that she had taken the lead instead of him. He was meant to be the Captain of this adventure and Captains never went last.

Jess turned and waved at him to catch up. 'Look I can see a path or animal track up ahead.' She pointed to what she had spotted. A thin line in the undergrowth had been marked out, where there was the slightest hint of path. 'I reckon we should see where it goes. If I think back to the map, it's roughly in the right direction. Look at those two trees it goes between. They are good markers for us. If it is an animal track though, we had better watch out for Rocket and make sure she doesn't run off chasing deer or anything.'

'Finn, where is Rocket?' asked Jess with a slight hint of worry in her voice.

'I don't know, I thought she was with you?' said Finn, who was getting a little fed up now with the whole situation of being spoken down to. 'She was with you, when we stopped at the tree back there.'

'Oh great, we've lost Rocket. That's just great.' muttered Jess looking around her with a pained expression on her face. 'We can't start shouting for her, it might alert someone we are here.'

'Who is going to be here?' said Finn trying to sound in charge.

'Err....Farmer Cramner. Or have you forgotten that he likes to walk around this area of the woods?' Jess whispered irritably.

They both stayed in the crouch position with their backs to each other in a huff, looking and listening for any sign of Rocket. For what felt like a very long time they waited patiently to see if she would return to them. Finn was beginning to wonder how he would explain to his parents that he had lost the family dog. This mini

89

adventure was not turning out the way he had hoped it would. How could it have gone wrong so quickly?

After a few minutes in silence, Jess turned to him.

'I'm sorry Finn, I just get carried away sometimes. I'll go back to the field if you want me to and see if Rocket has gone back there to wait for us?'

'I don't think it's good to split up,' said Finn, realising that this was the first command he had given that wasn't disagreed with; perhaps Jess truly was sorry. 'Rocket will find us, let's go on a bit and see if we can see anything interesting. Just a short way, remember we are going to come back here tomorrow. Stay close.' He gave Jess a tug on her sleeve as he moved off as if to say he was sorry for the way he had been too.

They crept slowly up the path Jess had seen and made their way deeper into the trees. The field was long gone now, and they were alone in the wood.

The path wound its way up a gentle slope with branches hanging over it. As Finn looked up, he could see sunlight trying to break through the woodland canopy. The light shimmered between the leaves and filtered down in beams to where he and Jess were stealthily working their way into the woodland. They quickly slipped back into explorer mode and it really felt as if they were discovering this path for the first time.

Every so often they would stop in a crouch and give each other a thumbs up. So far, so good, there was no sign of Farmer Cramner and their adventure was back on track. Except that they had lost Rocket, but Finn knew she always came back eventually. Rocket would be just as excited as them, he told himself. It was her chance to explore this new paradise of smells and sniffs!

Jess and Finn carried on following the path. The further they went, the more exciting it became. They had become quite efficient in moving silently, even with their wellies on.

Up ahead, the path began to climb a gentle slope and more light shone through the trees. Finn pulled Jess into a crouch and whispered.

'This is good Jess; the path is going uphill. I think this might lead us all the way to the spot where the castle is? Castles were always built on hills so they were difficult to attack. The castle might not be too much further.'

'Good, I don't think we should go for much longer Finn. I'm starting to get nervous,' gulped Jess.

'Don't worry, let's see what's at the top of the hill, it's only up there, come on.' Finn moved off quickly, eager to get up to the top and see what was on the other side. As they climbed the rise, they had to use their hands to scramble up the path as it got steeper. Finn imagined himself as a scout for an invading army who had been sent behind enemy lines to see what he could find.

As they reached the top of the hill, they both crawled on their bellies, not wanting to be seen by anyone as they looked down over the ridge. Very slowly they raised their heads, and their breath was taken away.

Roughly a hundred paces from where they were lying was a medieval castle. The very same castle they had seen in the book. The castle pictured on the treasure map.

In each corner there was a large tower covered in ivy with arrow slits and windows. In places, parts of the walls had crumbled and they could see into the courtyard beyond. Directly in front of them was the gate house and keep where the huge doorway and portcullis would have been. It was as if the castle had stood still in time. The birds and animals of the woodland had been allowed to take it over, its secret location and history lost to nature.

Both children couldn't speak. They just lay there, propped up on their elbows with their mouths hanging open in complete amazement.

'Wow....' they both whispered to each other. 'This is unbelievable,' said Finn.

'We've found it!' exclaimed Jess.

'I can't believe that we didn't know this was here. A proper medieval castle in the woods behind the farm. Just think of who has visited this place. What secrets does it hold? It's a treasure in itself,' said Finn. 'We can't go any further now. We have to get back and find Rocket.'

'At least we know how to get here tomorrow' said Jess as she slithered backwards down the hill. Finn couldn't resist one last look at the magnificent castle before he ducked his head down and made it back to the path.

Both children retraced their steps the way they had come. Having found the castle, they felt more confident than ever being in the woods. Finn and Jess both giggled with pure excitement as they jogged down the path that led towards the field, their wellies making a clacking noise as they ran. This meant they missed the noise of someone walking through the bushes near them. It wasn't until a big branch suddenly moved several feet away that they stopped dead in their tracks.

Immediately, Finn knew it could only be one person walking around in the woods. He grabbed Jess as quickly as he could and they both hid behind the nearest tree. Whoever it was continued to thrash their way through the undergrowth. They could hear branches being snapped, bushes and small trees were moving from side to side. It sounded as if something was being dragged through the trees. Whatever it was didn't care about how much noise it was making. How could he have been so stupid not to take more care, Finn thought to himself. If they got caught now, they would be in serious trouble. The noise was getting closer to their hiding place. Finn and Jess had never remained so still in all their lives, they didn't even want to blink.

And then the noise stopped.

Had they been seen? Why had it suddenly gone so quiet? Nothing could be heard, not even the birds in the trees. Someone or something was waiting for them to move. Jess turned her head very slowly to Finn and gulped. The look in her wide eyes told him everything he needed to know in how she was feeling.

Jess mouthed the words 'Is it Rocket?'

In slow motion, Finn put his finger to his lips and shook his head in answer to her question. There is no way Rocket could make that much noise Finn thought to himself.

They waited and waited.

Just when Finn thought he was about to get cramp in his leg because of the way he was crouched down, the noise started again and to their great relief it sounded as if it was moving in a different direction, away from them.

Finn strained to listen to what on earth could be making such a racket as it made its way through the bushes and trees. When the sound had gone, Jess squeezed his hand and whispered.

'Let's get out of here Finn, I'm really scared, what was making that noise?' With that, Jess darted out from behind the tree and dragged Finn after her. They scuttled along the path, stopping every so often to make sure they couldn't hear anything. At last, the field came into view and to their great relief, Rocket was sitting at the edge of the woods waiting for them. She gave them a 'I told you so' look and welcomed them back with a few small happy barks.

Finn leapt up over the bushes to land in the warm lush grass. Never had he been so grateful to be back in the open field again. Jess was hugging Rocket and talking to her in short bursts.

'Good girl Rocky ...I knew you would be waiting for us...... I was so worried about you...Where did you go?...Were you scared? I was scared but I'm not now.... Good girl.'

Finn turned to stare back into the woods from where they had come. What was it making that noise? Could it have been Farmer Cramner if he was dragging something? But what would he have been dragging? How did they manage not to get spotted making all that noise coming down the path? Or had they been spotted?

He breathed a sigh of relief that both he, Jess and Rocket were safe. The castle felt like a dream and to know that it was there hidden in the woods made him tingle with excitement. The thought of having to go back in there having heard that noise made him nervous, but he knew he had to go and try and find the treasure. Anyway, things felt better now. The sun was shining. Rocket was with them and they had found the castle. As they began to head down to the farm, Finn looked back once more in the dark woods, he had that funny feeling that someone or something was watching and waiting for them. For some reason the message on the bottom of the treasure map came into his head. 'Beware of the treasure, beware who guards the treasure.'

Chapter 11. The day they had been waiting for

Finn lay in bed that night going over everything that had happened to him in the last couple of days. It had already been a whirlwind of excitement and adventure. His midnight trip to Buckland Farm seemed a long time ago. The moonlight shone through his open window and onto the treasure map he held in his hands. Once again, Finn stared at it, trying to solve some of the many unanswered questions it threw at him. Who drew this map? Why was it ripped out of the book? How did it get to Buckland Farm?

To think, Jess and he had actually found the castle where it said treasure could be found.

What would tomorrow bring he wondered? Jess had seemed keen to go back to the woods early in the morning.

'All that noise, it must have been a big deer, that's all. We must have startled it with all the noise we were making. It was probably more scared of us than we were of him,' she had said. 'Now we know how to get to the castle, we can be there in no time. Let's go first thing after breakfast. I can't wait to explore.'

Finn loved the fact he didn't have to go back into the woods on his own. He was worried Jess might have been scared off. Especially after the look she had given him when they were hiding behind the tree.

Still, at least this time they could be more prepared. It was going to be much easier to move in trainers compared to their wellies. They would take some food and drink in a backpack, the treasure map and a torch, just in case. He couldn't think of anything else they would need. Perhaps a lead for Rocket in case that deer came back again. As Finn snuggled down in his duvet, he carefully placed the treasure map back into the book and got his pillow just how he liked it. In a matter of moments, he was breathing deeply and dreaming of treasure found in long lost castles.

The next morning, Finn and Jess were up early. It felt like it was going to be a special day. It had that feeling in the air that something was going to happen. It was a mixture of nerves and 'excited tinglyness' as Finn had described it whilst wolfing a big bowl of his favourite cereal. Nothing tasted better to Finn than a bowl of cereal with ice cold milk. The bright early sunshine gave them an extra spring in their step as they made their way through the farmyard to the fields.

Jess was wearing her favourite blue dungarees for the adventure and insisted on carrying the rucksack with the picnic and torch. Rocket could sense something was up and she bounced around having her own doggy 'tinglyness' moments.

The rooks cawed to each other high up in trees as the three intrepid adventurers wound their way up the field to the spot where they had left the woods only the previous afternoon. With every step they became more confident.

'I wonder what the castle is called?' said Jess. 'It must have a name. I'm surprised it wasn't called something in that book we found. What are the woods called? Do they have a name?'

'I don't know.... they have always just been called the woods by us,' responded Finn as he went to kick the head off a dandelion, sending hundreds of small white parachutes floating into the warm morning air.

They stood at the top of the field and Finn glanced over to where he had first spotted the balloon caught in the hedge. Everything he had gone through had led them to this point. Finally, he would get to investigate what this whole mystery was all about. He took a deep breath and stepped into the cool shaded world of the woods.

The path was easy to find and he even found a white piece of paper that he had dropped the previous day. He picked it up and smiled to himself. They didn't need a paper trail now. They knew where to go. Rocket stayed close to them as they retraced their steps along the path towards the castle.

As they walked, they were careful not to make too much noise. They didn't want to disturb any deer or bump into Farmer Cramner. Finn still couldn't work out why he had seen him driving down to Buckland Farm in the middle of the night.

It wasn't long before they made it to the place where they had realised they had lost Rocket yesterday. The two tall tress towered above them and acted as a gateway to the castle path. Jess decided it would be a good idea to put Rocket on the lead so she couldn't run off again.

'I think we should only talk in hushed whispers from now on.' said Finn. 'If we get split up for any reason, then let's meet back here at these trees. They seem to be a good marker and it is easy to find our way back to the field from here. Are you going to keep Rocket?'

'Yes, I don't mind having her. Okay, these trees then,' said Jess looking around. 'But Finn, why would we get split up? I don't fancy being in the woods on my own. Can we stay together?'

'Of course, we can, I just think it's good to have a place we can meet up if need be.'

Finn looked at Jess and tried to give her a reassuring smile. She looked a little worried and wasn't quite as carefree as she had been on the way up.

The path started to climb uphill towards the ridge that looked over to the castle. Butterflies began to flutter in their stomachs, and everything seemed to sound a little louder, including their own heartbeat in their ears. Finn told himself it was good to feel nervous, as it made it more exciting.

They climbed the steep path in the same way they had done yesterday and could see the marks they had left in the mud from their previous scramble. Rocket made easy work of the hill and was the first to step onto the ridge pulling Jess up the last bit with the lead. Finn scrambled up and once more his breath was taken away by the sight of the castle. It seemed to look even more mysterious in the morning sunshine. There was a light breeze ruffling the tops of the trees and occasionally it found its way down onto the woodland floor. As Finn and Jess stared at the castle, the wind whistled its ghostly whisper around the walls. The ivy swished backwards and forwards like coral as if the castle was underwater in the sea.

This time, Finn and Jess didn't just stop on the ridge, they continued to make their way up to the castle entrance. Finn tried to imagine what it would have felt like if he was riding on a huge war horse coated in armour.

'Shall we go through the gate?' asked Jess, tilting her head back and looking up at the battlements towering above them. Every so often a bird would fly out of an upstairs window where it had made its home.

'Let's go around the walls and see what else there is to explore before we go inside,' replied Finn as he began to carefully make his way to the left of the gatehouse. Stones lay scattered like graves on the slope from where they had fallen off the top of the ramparts. It wasn't as easy as Finn thought it would be to go around the walls.

They had to climb over branches, avoid falling into large patches of stinging nettles and the worst of all were the huge thorns on the brambles. Bit by bit, they made their way around the castle wall.

All the time Finn had an ear out for any unusual noise. Thankfully, there was no sign of Farmer Cramner. He knew Rocket would hear anything before he or Jess did.

'Rocky, be sure to give us a warning growl if you hear anything strange' whispered Finn to reassure himself. Rocket looked at him and then bounced down the next bit, making it look easy.

As the two of them kept making their way around the edge of the wall, the whole time feeling the history of the place soak through them, they came to a spot where the wall had fallen down enough for them to see into the courtyard. Weeds and bushes had grown up all around the centre of the castle and there were even trees growing up against the walls.

'Where do you think the treasure is?' Jess asked. The two of them were so excited about discovering the castle that they had almost forgotten there was also treasure to find.

'I don't know, the map just marks the castle as where the treasure is hidden. It could be anywhere?'

'Shall we climb over the broken wall here and go into the castle?' I am dying to go and explore inside.'

'I think we should keep heading round and go through the main gate. We don't know how safe that wall is, and I wouldn't want us to hurt ourselves if it starts to crumble more.' Finn pointed to the spot Jess was talking about. He would normally be the one to take risks but for some reason today he didn't want to do anything that could lead them into any harm.

Rocket led them back round to the gatehouse and they found themselves looking into the shadows of the castle entrance. It was one thing to skirt around the edge of the walls, now it was about going into the castle for real.

'You ready?' said Finn nervously as he grabbed Jess's hand. They both stood there looking into the dark hole of the castle doorway.

'Ready as I'll ever be' said Jess with a squeeze of his hand. 'Let's go and find the treasure.'

Just as they were about to move they heard a noise that sent shivers down their spines and rooted them to the spot. Rocket pricked up her ears and started growling. Deep in the woods they could hear dogs barking.

Chapter 12. 'Come on…RUN'

Panic rushed through Finn's body. Jess let out a small scream and grabbed hold of Finn. Had they been seen crawling around the castle wall? They can't have been, this place seemed deserted. Rocket continued to growl and she bared her teeth, snarling at the horrific screeching noise coming from the woods below the castle. The hairs on her back were standing up on end and that sight alone was enough to scare Finn. Rocket never acted like this.

The noise of the dogs barking was getting closer. It sounded like two or maybe three large dogs howling their way towards them.

'Hang on, I thought dad said that Farmer Cramner doesn't have any dogs?'

'We have to get out of here Finn, where can we go?' Jess wailed. The peace and calm of the wood had been shattered in seconds and turned into a savage storm of fear. Rocket was barking with everything she had. She was straining on her lead, tossing her head from side to side. Jess was doing everything to hold on to her.

'Rocket stop pulling…. I can't keep hold….' Jess didn't get a chance to finish her sentence. Rocket had slipped her collar and broken free and she was hurtling away towards the noise of the barking dogs. Jess was left holding her lead with her collar attached to it. Just as Rocket reached the small ridge, she turned back to look at Finn and Jess before darting into the undergrowth.

'ROCKET....ROCKET.... COME BACK!' yelled Finn. He knew what could happen if she met those dogs in a fight.

'What will those dogs do to her?' cried Jess as she grabbed onto Finn again. Rocket's barks could be heard as she charged away from the castle.

Finn could do nothing to help Rocket now. He grabbed Jess's hand and ran into the shadows of the castle gatehouse. They had to find somewhere to hide quickly. Those dogs would be here in no time. Finn let go of Jess and ran.

'COME ON...RUN!' he shouted over his shoulder in desperation without even looking back. He sprinted across the courtyard dodging the stones and bushes to get away from the horrific noise of the dogs. Further into the castle he ran, he could see the walls rising up around him. There must be a place to hide? He looked ahead of him to one of the towers in the corner. That's where he'd go. Up into the tower. Just as Finn got to the doorway, he turned to see how Jess was getting on.

Jess wasn't there. She was nowhere to be seen. Where was she? This was turning into a nightmare. First, he had lost Rocket and goodness know what would happen when Rocket came face to face with those big dogs. Now, Jess had vanished.

'JESS....JESSICA!' he roared so it echoed around the inner walls. There was no reply. All that he could hear was the barking getting closer. He had to hide.

Finn looked back into the tower and saw steps leading up. He had to try and get up them. It was his only hope. There were brambles and stinging nettles up to his waist blocking his way. He had no choice but to leap as far as he could through the tower doorway and was immediately caught in the thorns. He hastily ripped them off his shorts as best he could and painfully swept his way onto the first stair. Scratches and cuts were least of his worries now. Where was Rocket? Where was Jess?

Up the spiral stairwell Finn bounded; his lungs were burning, and he could feel his heart racing. This was not the adventure he had wanted. The old smooth stone stairs wound their way up to the first floor and stopped. He reached the doorway. In front of him where the floor should have been was an empty space, he swayed dangerously over the edge but managed to grab on to the side just before he lost his balance. Far below him was a thick deadly stew of brambles and nettles. Finn could see most of the courtyard through the tower windows. He realised he was not safe. The dogs could still get to him. He had to move further away from these stairs.

As he looked into the empty tower, he realised that there were still stones jutting out of the walls where the floor had once been. If he was careful, he could step out onto the stones and make his way around the edge of the room. It was his only chance. Sliding himself out of the doorway and keeping his back against the cold stone wall, he was able to step onto the first jutting out stone. Finn dared not look down, he held his breath as he put all his weight onto it. It held him, and he exhaled slowly with his eyes shut. Looking sideways, he could see the next stone to stand on. He reached out with his foot and shuffled himself along before he stepped out once more. Again, the stone held him and he was making progress around the edge of the room.

Just then, three enormous dogs charged through the gatehouse entrance, snarling and howling with their barks sounding even louder as they echoed around the castle ruins. They were just the sort of dogs to scare people with. Terrifying black muscled beasts that were the size of a small horse. They picked up Finn and Jess's scent and began following their noses, stopping every so often to look around them and smell the air.

Finn could see the dogs below and knew it was only a matter of time before they found him. He had managed to make it onto a window ledge and was holding onto a branch from a tree that poked its way into the room. Only now did he realise how much was shaking with fear. He sat on the ledge gripping tightly to the branch trying to work out a way out of this nightmare. He just wanted to be back in the field with Rocket and Jess. He didn't care about the treasure anymore, he just wanted to be safe.

The dogs stopped their chase in the courtyard and began barking at something on the ground. Finn couldn't see what had caught their attention as bushes and grass were scattered over the area, but whatever it was made them bark wildly.

The barking seemed to go on and on, the three dogs frantically gnarling at whatever it was on the floor. Then Finn realised, it must be Jess they are barking at there must be a hole in the ground. She must have fallen down the hole when she was running across the yard. Oh, poor Jess. I hope she is okay and hasn't hurt herself.

Finn thought about calling out to her but then what good would that do? She probably wouldn't hear him over the noise of the barking and if he did shout then that would only let the dogs know he was hiding in the tower. He was stuck.

Chapter 13. 'Jess where are you?'

The longer Finn sat on the window ledge, the more he realised there was no one coming to help him or Jess. Down below in the castle yard, the dogs had given up barking. They stalked around the hole growling viscously.

He sat on the ledge tucked into a ball. His knees were pulled up tight to his chest and he hugged them with his other arms. Despite the warm day, he felt cold and shivered with fear. Tears streamed down his cheeks, he couldn't even be bothered to wipe them away and they dripped down onto his muddy knees. He didn't normally cry; he wasn't even sure exactly what he was crying about. Was it the fear of the dogs, or the fact he'd let Jess get into trouble, or was it because his dream of finding the treasure was gone?

Through his tear-soaked eyes he saw the dogs turn and growl at the open space in the courtyard wall.

The growls became fiercer as they paced towards the crumbled down stones.

What could be making the dogs growl now? Finn watched the gap in the wall wondering what would happen next.

Suddenly he saw a sight that made his heart jump for joy; Rocket was standing on top of the stones.

'Rocket!' exclaimed Finn, as he brushed away his tears. He could see her standing tall, she was safe and had come back.

No sooner had she appeared in the gap then she was gone again. The three black dogs leapt after her and disappeared over the stones through the gap in the wall in a wave of fury and rage.

Finn smiled to himself. There was hope. Rocket had come back. He knew then what he had to do. He had to show the same bravery as Rocket. It was down to him now to get them out of this mess. Finn stood up on the ledge carefully but bumped his head on the branch. As he rubbed the painful spot, the idea came to him as to how he could get out of the tower. He could try and climb down the tree that the branch was attached to. It was going to be seriously dangerous and would use all his tree climbing skill, but he thought it was probably safer than trusting his weight on those old stones again. He managed to squeeze himself out of the small window holding onto the branch tightly with both his hands. Thankfully the branch was strong and would easily take his weight. Finn didn't look down. He knew how high up he was, and it wouldn't help him to see the woodland floor spinning beneath him. With one last big breath, he dropped his legs down and began climbing along the branch by placing hand over hand. His legs dangled beneath, swinging wildly in the air. With all his might, he worked his way along the branch. He could feel his muscles and strength fading. A few more handholds and at last he found himself placing his feet onto a lower branch to take the weight off his aching limbs. He was still a long way up in the tree but the hardest part was over.

As he stopped to get his breath back, he could hear the birds begin to chirp and the gentle sound of the woodland was restored. Gone was the evil barking noise. The castle was returned to its silent abandoned state.

It didn't take Finn long to climb down the tree. He was well practised in finding good lookout posts at the tops of the trees on the farm. He had never climbed down a tree at the side of castle before though.

Finn remembered the route around the wall that he and Jess had discovered earlier. In no time, he was scrambling up the same stones that Rocket had as he made his way to the gap in wall. Earlier, he had said to Jess he didn't think they should go over that spot. Not this time, he needed to get into the courtyard as quickly as he could.

Ever since he managed to climb along the branch and down the tree, Finn felt more alive than ever. He was bumped and scraped all over, but that didn't matter. He had only one thought in his mind, which was to find Jess.

There was no noise of any dogs and Finn wondered where Rocket had gone. Had she been able to get away?

As he clambered down the last few stones into the castle yard, his eyes were fixed on the area where the dogs had been. Sure enough, as he crept closer he could see a dark opening in the ground. This must have been what Jess fell into. Maybe this was the old dungeon? The stones around the edge of the gaping hole looked loose and he didn't want to risk falling in himself.

'Jess... Jess....can you hear me? Are you okay...? Jess?' said Finn gently. He leaned over as far as he could to stare down into the hole. It was black and murky, he couldn't see anything. Daylight tried its best to stream down into the darkness but all it could manage was to light up swirls of dust, spinning around sleepily. There was no way of knowing how deep it was. He couldn't just jump down.

'Jess...it's me Finn. Are you alright? Finn listened for anything; nothing. No sound came back to him, all he could hear were the birds calling to each other high up in the trees.

What was he to do? Jess must be down there. He had to try and find her.

'Think Finn, think,' he muttered to himself. 'Think,' there must be something he could do. He looked around the castle yard to see if there was any other way to get down underground. There must have been secret passages and tunnels all over this castle at one time he thought.

Judging from where the sun was in the sky, Finn could tell it was near midday. He had been in the tower a lot longer than he realised. He didn't feel hungry though, his nerves made sure of that. At least he still had time to try and find Jess. His parents weren't expecting them back until much later.

Finn thought about going to find his mum and dad and tell them what had happened. But that would only cause lots of worry and he also felt bad that he had lied to them, saying they were going fishing. No, he wanted to sort this out himself. But if he couldn't find her in the next hour then he promised himself he would have to go and tell his dad. As hard as that would be.

As Finn thought things through, he walked around the hole peering down for any sign of Jess. The castle ruins looked down on him in silent judgement.

'There must be another way down,' he said to himself, kicking a small stone in frustration. He put his hands in his pockets and felt the folds of the treasure map. 'Of course, how stupid of me.' Finn pulled the map out and unfolded it. His eyes immediately went to the area where he had seen the dark circle about a finger's width from the castle. It could be a tunnel?! The dotted line along the map leads to the castle. He realised the tunnel could lead him underneath the castle to Jess.

Chapter 14. There must be another way down there?

'Jess....Jess...if you can hear me, I think I might have found a way down to you. I am going to try and find the tunnel that we saw on the treasure map. I hope you are okay.... stay there, I'm coming.' Finn sounded a lot braver than he actually felt as he half whispered, half spoke the words down into the hole.

He turned and listened to see if there was any sign of the dogs. Rocket must have run them miles from here. What a good girl she was. Finn knew Rocket could run faster and further than any dog around. He was so proud of her. With a renewed purpose and a hope of finding Jess, Finn scrambled back up through the gap in the wall in the direction he thought the tunnel started. He kept his map in his left hand to look back at it every so often to check he was heading in the right direction. The new area of woodland he was in looked the same as the track from the field. He remembered his mother's warning about getting lost and concentrated even harder. He was trying to go in a straight line from almost exactly the middle of the castle yard. It wasn't always easy to do as trees and bushes meant he had to climb around them, but he always made sure he was on the same line as best he could.

Finn was making good progress and looked back to see the castle ruins through the trees. It wouldn't be long before he was in the place where the map said the tunnel was.

He was just about to turn and carry on, when his attention was caught by a figure in the castle yard. Someone was standing looking into the hole, exactly where Finn had been only a few moments earlier. Finn ducked down and pulled a branch across himself to hide. The figure shuffled around and looked directly through the gap in the wall towards Finn.

Farmer Cramner didn't move, he just stood there and stared. Finn was too far away to see the expression on his face, but he knew he couldn't move. As this strange staring contest carried on, Finn realised that he must have come to find his dogs. Perhaps he was walking with them in the woods when they ran had run off?

This was the last thing Finn needed, it was going to be hard enough to find Jess, let alone having to worry about a grumpy Farmer Cramner in the castle.

Finally, the fat shape of Cramner shuffled away from the opening in the wall, and Finn was able to breathe a sigh of relief. He was pretty sure he hadn't been seen, if only Farmer Cramner would go back to where he came from, now he knew his dogs weren't in the castle.

Finn turned again and scurried off in search of the tunnel. He jumped down into a small ditch that faced a slab of rock covered in moss and ivy. Feeling the mud squidge beneath him as he landed. According to the map, this was where the tunnel was meant to start. As Finn stood there looking at the map, trying to work out where it could be, he felt a cold draft waft against his legs. His legs hairs stood on end as the cool air surrounded him.

Looking up slowly from the map, his eyes widened. The slap of rock covered in ivy was moving. The ivy was gently swaying from the bottom up. Finn stepped forward and pushed his hand past the green plant leaves. Where there was meant to be rock was cold, moist air. This was it; he had found the secret tunnel. Finn delicately pulled the ivy back to reveal a black hole leading into the hill side. There was no way of seeing how far it went as after the first few yards it pitched into darkness. Water was dripping with strange sounds echoing down the tunnel as the drops fell onto the puddled floor. The tunnel smelt of green damp wetness.

With his heart beating fast, Finn folded up the map to put in his pocket, his eyes caught by the words at the bottom:

'Beware of the treasure. Beware of who guards the treasure. Beware to use the treasure wisely or the same fate awaits you.'

He pulled the ivy away from the tunnel entrance to get as much light into it as possible. If only I had the torch with me, thought Finn. Jess has it in the ruck sack. Maybe she has been able to use it?

Finn squinted into the darkness and began to take his first squelching steps along the secret tunnel. He ran his hand down the slimy moss-covered wall as he walked. Even though it was wet and cold, he felt comfort knowing where the side was. For some reason, he wasn't as scared as he thought he would be. Too much had happened to him already today. He knew he had to go down the tunnel to help Jess, there was no other way.

After what seemed to be a very short time, Finn found himself in complete darkness. He could put his hand in front of his face and see nothing. The drips from the ceiling sounded eerily loud as his shoes were becoming wetter with each step. The cold water was oozing into his socks. Every so often a drip would land on his neck and slither down his back.

How much further did he have to go he wondered? This felt so strange, walking through an underground tunnel to the castle.

As Finn made his way along, he began to make out shapes in the darkness. Mysterious sounds came along the passageway and Finn almost thought he could hear a human voice. Was it Jess? Perhaps being so long underground in the darkness made his mind play tricks on him. But no, there it was again. The low murmuring noise, a deep booming sound. Finn stopped and listened. The drips from the ceiling made it hard to hear but he could definitely make out noises.

Where were they coming from? If he kept on walking would he reach the sounds? So many thoughts were rushing through his mind. He tried to blank out the constant questions, but he couldn't. Where was Rocket? What did the map mean 'Beware of who guards the treasure' Was Farmer Cramner still up in the castle courtyard?

And then his thoughts and questions were suddenly interrupted by what Finn had been waiting to hear in a long, long time; Jess's voice was coming from down the tunnel.

Finn shut his eyes and tilted his head back in pure relief. Drips splattered onto his face, but he didn't care, as he could hear Jess was alright. But hang on, who was she talking to? It can't be Farmer Cramner. Who on earth was Jess talking to?

Finn just couldn't understand what was going on. There was someone else down here with them? He began to move faster along the tunnel towards the noises. His eyes started to pick out shapes as darkness changed into a dim murky light. The light must be coming from the hole in the courtyard, Finn realised. Where was Jess? She must be close by?

'Jess....Can you hear me? It's Finn...I'm down here in a tunnel....Where are you?' whispered Finn urgently. He strained to see further.

'Finn...is that you?' called Jess anxiously.

'Yes...I'm coming down a tunnel. I can't see anything properly, it is all so dark. Where are you? Are you okay, I've been so worried!'

Finn kept walking towards the light and, bit by bit, his eyes were adjusting.

'Jess....where are you? Can you see me, it sounds like you are talking to someone? What's going on? Is there someone else down here?'

Jess could hear Finn coming down the tunnel in front of her. Her eyes had grown used to the dim light and despite everything, she was in good spirits. This next bit was going to be very difficult for Finn to understand.

'Finlay.....Finlay......I want you to keep walking towards the light. I can hear your footsteps in the tunnel. Please keep looking at me until I explain what's going on. Finlay, you must keep looking at me, do you understand?' Jess made sure she said this very slowly as if she was talking to a young child. She hoped that he would notice she used his full name and that would make him listen and follow her instructions.

Immediately Finn understood what Jess had meant. This made him nervous that something was wrong. She sounded okay though, why did she want him to keep looking at her?

Finn stumbled out into a large cave, he could the light beams shining down form the courtyard in the distance. His eyes were still getting used to it all, but he could make out the silhouette of Jess standing up slowly and walking towards him.

Jess was speaking to him and pointing for him to keep looking at her, but his attention was drawn by something to his left. Finn turned his head slowly to see what it was.

He could hear Jess shout at him to look at her and then he realised why. In the fraction of a second, Finn remembered the drawing he had seen on the desk in Buckland Farm. In the corner of the cave was a dragon.

Chapter 15. The biggest surprise of all

Finn fainted in surprise right there on the spot. Thankfully, Jess had worked out that this was probably going to be the case, as the same thing had happened to her right after she had fallen down the hole. Jess was able to grab him and gently lay him down on the floor using the backpack as a pillow.

'Do you think he's going to be okay?' a voice boomed out from the spot Finn had turned to look at.

'I hope so, I know he likes surprises but that was just a little bit too big for him,' said Jess. 'And it's not every day that you walk down a dark tunnel under a castle to find a dragon at the end of it!'

'No, I suppose it's not,' replied the dragon in a deep, gravelly tone. 'You didn't faint for long though after you landed on me. I was having a nice snooze until you fell through that hole over there.' The dragon swished his tail in the direction of the light beams shining down from the courtyard. He then rested his large head onto his front claws. Jess smiled and realised he reminded her of how a dog sits down in front of a warm fire.

'The next thing I need to work out is how I explain to him that you're a friendly dragon and you talk. I really hope he doesn't freak out when he wakes up!' Jess looked at Finn and could see the treasure map hanging out of the pocket of his shorts. She grabbed it and had an idea.

'Here, let me show you this' said Jess as she went over to where the dragon was resting. His large eyes studied what she was carrying, and he lifted his head up.

'Hang on, I don't think I can see it here, it's too dark, let's go over to the light coming in from the courtyard hole.'

'If you insist,' droned the dragon in a sleepy voice.

With that, the dragon slowly hefted his weight onto his back legs and waddled carefully past the fainted Finn. The dragon's enormous tail swished long the floor, sending clouds of dust up into the air.

Jess was already below the hole. She had placed the map on the floor in a patch of light and sat cross legged, studying the strange piece of paper. The dragon peered over her shoulder and gave a snort. Jess could feel his heavy breath on her neck. His bowling ball eyes blinked at the same time and it was if he was smiling.

'So young Finn found the map where I put it, good lad. I have waited a long time to see this piece of paper again.' The dragon's voice boomed around his underground home. Every time he spoke, the place seemed to shake and tremble.

'What do you mean, you put it there?' said Jess as she looked up and wished she hadn't as all she could see were two large dark dragon nostrils.

'I think I will wait until young Finn is awake and I will explain all to you both, it will be easier that way. Look

121

there is the tunnel that Finn has just come down.' The dragon delicately placed a single claw on the map and pointed to the dark hole that Finn had found.

'What do all these symbols mean down the side here?' said Jess. 'We couldn't work them out.'

'Can you tell us what the words mean at the bottom, is there really treasure here in the castle? I think I know what it means when it says, 'beware of who guards the treasure.' The dragon gave another short snort and Jess realised this was the sound when he laughed a little.

'All in good time Jessica, now let us see how your friend is getting on, he must be awake soon.' The dragon plodded his feet around in a circle and looked back to where Finn was lying.

'Oh dear, it looks like he is about to get a visit from my little friends, this will give him another shock!'

'I can't move his head......it's just too heavy....'

'What do you mean, you can't move his head? I'm the one trying to move the heavy thing. This bag just won't shift. I know there is going to be yummy food in here, why else would they have brought it?'

'Would you please stop thinking about your stomach, just for one moment?'

'No, I'm hungry and I can smell the food from here. If you would just keep trying to move his head I think I can squeeze into the top of the bag.'

'Yes, but what happens when you squeeze in the bag and start eating all the food? I won't get any cos I'm stuck up here trying to shift his heavy head!'

'Oh, so who's thinking about their stomach now then?'

'Oooh, I think he might be waking up, get up here, I think he is just about to open his eyes'

The little mouse abandoned her struggle of trying to get into the bag and jumped up on to Finn's chest next to the other mouse. Both mice stared at Finn's eyelids as they started to flicker.

'What are you doing sticking your tongue out at him?' said one mouse to the other. 'Can't you see that this poor boy has had a most dreadful fright after seeing old dragon breath over there, the last thing he wants to see when he wakes up is to see you sticking your tongue out at him.'

'Oh, I thought it might cheer him up' said the other mouse. 'Look I can even cross my eyes at the same time, look.' The mouse turned with her eyes crossed and tongue sticking out the side of her mouth.

'Sometimes, I really do wonder if we are related, you know,' tutted the other mouse. 'Now look, his eyes are definitely trying to open.'

Finn could hear small voices and felt tiny feet scrambling on his chest before he opened his eyes. He had that strange feeling of not having a clue where he actually was. His mind felt groggy and everything was happening in slow motion. He blinked his eyes. Hang on, was that two small mice standing on his chest looking at him intently? He shut his eyes and opened them again. Was he hearing things or were the mice actually talking? He must be in one of those weird dreams where he thinks he is he awake but really, he is still tucked up in bed asleep at home.

As the seconds passed, Finn began to remember all that had happened to him. The hazy dream was becoming real. He could feel the cold floor on his legs. He smelt the murky, musty stink of the cavern. There were definitely two mice standing on him and he was awake enough to see that one had its tongue out.

'AAAAAAARRRRRRRGGGGGGGGHHHHHHHH!'   Finn shouted and sat up stiffly but not before the two mice had jumped off and retreated to a safe distance.

'Right, that's it, we are going to have to fight him for the food' said the mouse putting her fists up with her tongue still hanging out.

'Don't be so stupid, how on earth are we going to fight him and would you please put your tongue away? It makes you dribble when you talk.'

Jess came bounding through from where she had been studying the map and flung her arms around Finn.

'Jess, what is going on? I feel so strange. There were these two mice standing on my chest and I could swear they were talking to each other?' Finn said sitting up and rubbing his eyes. 'The last thing I remember was I thought I saw a creature that looked exactly like a dragon in the corner over there......What is going on?'

'Finn, there is no easy way to say this but.... you did see a dragon.' Jess was kneeling up in front of him, looking into his eyes and put a hand on his shoulder. 'I fainted exactly like you did, when I saw him for the first time having fallen through that hole, but it's okay. The dragon is friendly, I know you are finding this hard to understand but he can also talk. Any animal in here can talk. It's magic.'

Finn looked at Jess as if she had gone mad. But he could see that she was completely serious and meant every word.

'How did you not hurt yourself when you fell all that way through the hole?' Finn asked with his head tilted to the side, still not sure what to think or believe.

'I landed on him! He was having a snooze and I landed on him. It was like falling onto a scalely rough cold bean bag. I stood up and fainted at once, just like you!'

'What happened then?' asked Finn.

'Well, I don't know really. I must have come round quite quickly, I sat up and he was there, talking to me. I didn't feel scared. He is a friendly dragon. I told him about the map and our adventure. He told me about the magic in the castle. I didn't really understand it all but he did say that animals can talk in this cave. I guess I just talked about you and how I hoped you would come to find me. I wasn't scared as I don't think dragons eat people.... Do they?' It was Jess's turn to tilt her head now and she suddenly looked very worried.

'No, not this dragon, this one doesn't eat people; never fancied it, you'll be glad to hear.'

Another strange snort echoed from the shadows as the dragon waddled towards them. He lurched from side to side as he placed his gigantic feet, his talons crunching into the soft earth. Finn went to back away, but Jess held him and gave him a squeeze to let him know it would be alright.

Finn's eyes couldn't have opened any wider as he took in the mythical but very real living creature, only a few paces away from him.

The dragon towered above them, it was easily the size of the biggest tractor on Finn's fathers farm. Its neck and legs were like tree trunks covered in plate sized scales. Huge razor-sharp talons spread out like knives on his feet. The tail swished as if it was a humongous serpent, flicking back and forth as he moved. Rows of teeth, like sharpened white skittles, protruded from his enormous mouth, while his black watery eyes shone in the darkness. His bluey-green scales rippled through his body as he wound his way back to the corner of his lair.

'Sorry to startle you both Jess and Finn. I don't get many visitors apart from those two pesky mice.' The dragon settled himself back down in the murky corner.

'What do you mean, pesky mice? You big blue lump of poo' said the mouse with his tongue out. There was a slight dribble of spit as the mouse spoke and it bounced up to the dragon with its fists ready for a fight.

The dragon looked down its nose and studied the tiny mouse standing in front of him. Through his fire breathing mouth, it blew a gentle blast of hot air over the mouse who immediately thought it was on fire.

'Ah, I'm burning, the evil dragon has set me on fire! Quick Pee Mouse do something. I'm burning! Fire...fire....I need the flames put out, we haven't got any water, arrragggh.... the dragon is breathing fire. Pee Mouse you must do something.... Do anything to stop the flames!, Pee Mouse you might have to pee on me!' The small mouse frantically ran around the floor in tiny circles, hoping and jumping with its paws in the air.

The other mouse stood watching with its hands on its hips, shaking its head.

'Let me introduce my two mouse friends, Pee Mouse and Poo Mouse. I named them so because it's all they seem to do. Everywhere they go, they leave a little trail of pee and poo. As you've probably gathered, Pee Mouse here inherited the brains of the family,' rumbled the dragon as it lay it's head down on the floor again.

The two mice scuttled off into a dark corner but not before the one he called Poo Mouse had run up to the dragon and stuck her tongue out and shook her fist. 'Just you wait Athelstan, I'll get you back.'

'Athelstan.....why did the mouse call you Athelstan? I know that name, I have heard it recently.' said Finn putting his hands to his head, suddenly trying to remember where he had heard it from.

The dragon looked at them sadly, sorrow shaped in the eyes.

'Well, I did say that I would explain it all to you Jess, didn't I. I think I should start at the beginning.'

Finn and Jess looked at each other, they were about to discover what this adventure was all about. Here they were listening to a dragon tell them about the magic of the castle and its treasure.

Chapter 16. Athelstan's story

The dragon looked at them and held them in his gaze.

'This is story of sadness, I'm afraid,' started the dragon in his deep rumbling voice. 'It all comes back to wanting too much and not realising what you have.'

Both children looked at him unsure what to think. This wasn't what they were expecting.

'I want you to imagine this castle hundreds of years ago. This was a place of happiness and joy. The castle was filled with people from servants to royal guests. On special occasions it was lit up with merriment and feasting, tournaments and hunting parties. There was more food and drink than you could possibly have dreamed. It is difficult to imagine that now, seeing it today, all crumbled and silent.' The dragon paused and Jess could see he was remembering those golden days.

'How long have you lived here?' said Jess quietly, breaking into his thoughts.

'All in good time, young lady. Now, where was I? Ah yes, the castle was one of the greatest castles in the land. Kings and queens would come to stay often, it was known throughout the kingdom. This brought it great riches as each time a king or queen stayed, they would leave a gift to the castle in way of saying thank you. The gifts and money given to the castle soon built up, so the treasure chests were overflowing with gold and precious jewels.'

'This is where I come into the story,' sighed the dragon; he turned his head slightly to the side so he wasn't looking at them, as if he was ashamed to continue.

'I was once in charge of the castle. I was one of the King's most trusted men. A baron and knighted by King Edward III. My name was Baron Athelstan of Buckland.'

Both children's mouths dropped open in amazement, they couldn't speak.

'To think that I lived in great luxury and had everything I could have wanted. And now, here I am, a lonely dragon, destined to hide for ever down here in a wet, dark cave.'

'What....what...happened?' stammered Finn as he regained his voice.

'Well, as I said at the start of this tale, I wanted too much and didn't realise what I had.'

'What do you mean?' asked Jess, already starting to feel sad for him.

'I'm sorry, I don't seem to be telling this very well. It has been a long time since I have spoken it to anyone.' The dragon lifted his head up to look at them. 'I was the Baron, put here by the King to look after his lands and host his family when they would come to visit. I oversaw everything as far as the eye could see.' The dragon paused looking into the distance. 'The problem was that I wanted more. I wanted more power, I wanted to be richer. I made the mistake of believing that if I had more,

I would be happier and so I hatched a plan to steal the castle treasure and run away.'

Finn and Jess were completely absorbed in what the dragon was saying; they didn't even notice the two mice scuttle around the side of them and head towards their ruck sack.

The dragon continued, 'So one night I decided to run away with as much treasure as I could carry. There was an almighty storm raging. Lightning lit up the sky with great flashes, thunder shook the earth. Trees were ripped out of the ground as if they were twigs, torrential rain fell in rivers from the sky, the wind howled and buffeted the castle walls. I thought it would provide the perfect cover for my escape. No one would want to follow me into such a storm.

I saddled up my horse with the intention of riding away on the track leading from the castle. My saddle bags were filled to the brim with gold and jewels. The only problem was that my horse was too scared of the lightning and thunder, he refused to move or go anywhere from the stable. I had no choice but to go on foot, so I loaded as many bags with treasure and set out through the woods.'

'What happened next?' Finn asked as he hung on to every word the dragon spoke.

'This is where I can tell you about the magic of the woodland and this castle.' The dragon moved his long neck and head to within a few feet of the children's faces.

Both children gasped as the dragon said this, their eyes opening wide.

'Magic has been around since the dawn of time, there is magic everywhere, you just need to know where to look. The magic in these woods was here long before the castle came to be, and the magic will be here forever.'

'I don't understand, what do you mean there is magic everywhere?' said Finn.

'You will find that sentence to be true in time, young Finn. Listen to my story and it might help you understand more.'

'I rushed from the castle, loaded with bags. The storm surged around me as I made my way through the woods. Little did I know that however hard I would try to escape, the ancient magic in the woodland was never going to let me. I was lost in the woods in the darkness of the storm and I didn't know which way to turn, and all because I thought I wanted more.'

'I stumbled and struggled through the woodland paths, not knowing which way to go. The treasure was weighing me down. I was soaked through, tired, cold and helpless. It was then that the magic chose to reveal itself to me. I found a small hidden cave I hadn't seen before and went to shelter from the storm inside it. I soon realised the cave had a passage leading from the back of it into the hill side. My curiosity made me follow the passage and I felt my way along it in the dark.'

Jess and Finn listened to every word the dragon said, they couldn't even blink.

'At the end of the passage, I could see a light, I made my way towards it, not knowing what I was doing and how this would change my world forever. The light was shining from a single white candle placed on a large rock in a round cave. The candle seemed to make a high-pitched humming noise and the flame was red. I walked towards the candle and stopped. I knew something was wrong, I had been lured into the cave by the magic. I turned to run but the passage I had come up was no more. It had disappeared to become rock. I became frantic and desperately searched for an exit to get back out into the storm and away from this mysterious place. There was no escape, there was no way out. The candlelight began to flicker and then it spoke to me.'

'What....the candle spoke?' asked Finn in barely a whisper.

'A voice came from the candle,' the dragon replied.

'Then what happened? What did the candle say?' Jess butted in.

'Shush Jess, let him tell us,' pleaded Finn, frustrated that she had interrupted.

Chapter 17. Where is the treasure?

The dragon lowered his head and looked at both of them with his huge watery eyes.

'This is the part where the magic told me of my fate for stealing the treasure. The voice that came from the flickering candle was soft and light, as if a bird was singing.'

It said, 'You, keeper of the castle, have disobeyed the ancient woodland magic. You will remain in the woodland and live, but not as you know it. Your time here is forever, except for one night every hundred years, you will return to human form.'

'That was all that was spoken. The candle then flickered out and I was left in complete darkness. I cried out for help, but no one could hear me.' The dragon rested his head on his tail that had swished its way round to his front.

'So how did you become a dragon?' asked Finn.

'The ancient magic dictates that every woodland and forest has a dragon watching over it. My crime of stealing the treasure turned me into that dragon. I have been the guardian of Buckland Wood for the last six hundred years. Time is something that means nothing to me anymore.'

'What, so every wood or forest has a dragon in it?' Jess asked quizzically.

'If the woodland or forest is old enough and the ancient magic dictates it to be, then yes, there is a dragon hidden, watching over it,' answered the dragon simply. Both children were amazed at his answer.

'You must have seen the small cloud like smoke hanging in the air over forests or woods. Or when walking along a track, you may have seen strange marks on the floor. You might have even heard a noise that made you wonder what it was...... Those are the signs of a dragon.'

'But Athelstan...can I call you Athelstan? I hope you don't mind... it is...., was, your name.' said Jess going slightly red with embarrassment. 'How did you change into a dragon and end up here under the castle?'

'No one has called me Athelstan for hundreds of years, apart from my mouse friends, not since I was baron here,' replied the dragon. He continued to rest his head sadly on his tail as he spoke.

'The ancient woodland magic turned me into a dragon. In the darkness, after the candle had gone out, I managed to find a different passageway from the one I had entered by. The passage led me deep into the hill side and I discovered there were secret passages everywhere. An underground spider web of tunnels all joined together. I entered the cave a human and crawled out a dragon. I have lived here ever since. I go out into the woods by that that dark passage that you came up

Finn. I sometimes like to spread my wings and fly at night over the woodland when no one can see me.'

Jess stared in wonder at his bluey green wings, to think that when she looked out of the farmhouse windows on starry nights, she could have seen him flying above the dark shadow of the wood.

'What happened to the treasure?' said Finn. Jess looked at him with a scowl. How could Finn be thinking about the treasure after Athelstan had told such a sad story of how he came to be a dragon.

'Ah, yes the treasure. The treasure that turned me into this. It is still here buried deep within the hill side. I have not told or shown anyone where it is for hundreds of years. There have been those who have tried to find it, but all have failed.'

'You mean, it's still here hidden, deep underground, down one of these passageways?' Finn's eyes lit up with desire at the thought of finding the gold and jewels.

'Have you not listened to anything that Athelstan has said?' replied Jess, turning to him in annoyance. 'Can't you see what his love of treasure has done to him?'

'I only wanted to ask as it's what brought us here in the first place Jess, you remember how excited you were when we set out this morning. The thought of finding the lost treasure was all we wanted,' said Finn in a defensive manner.

'Yes, but look how much we have learnt since arriving here. I don't want to take any treasure away from the woodland if it means I am going to turn into a dragon.

The whole point of Athelstan telling us his story is to warn us to stay away from it. We have to learn from what has happened to him.' Jess turned to the dragon and spoke softly. 'That is right isn't it Athelstan? You wouldn't want us to find the treasure. It is meant to stay here in the woodland, near the castle.'

'You are wise for one so young, dear Jess,' responded the dragon; he lifted his head and nodded. 'It is true the treasure must remain a secret or the ancient curse will be put upon the finder. The only exception to the rule set in the ancient magic is if the person taking the treasure does not seek to gain or benefit from it in anyway.' The dragon lowered its head again and shut his eyes.

Finn and Jess didn't know what to say. They stared at the dragon and felt sorry for him. The treasure was there to find still, but the curse would be upon them if they took it and used it to make them rich.

'Hang on a minute,' said Finn. 'There is still lots I don't understand. So, you were turned into a dragon and have left the treasure hidden in a secret tunnel under the castle. But you said that once every hundred years you turn back into a human for one night, 'why don't you escape, away from the woodland on that night?'

'I have thought about it many times, but I find my place is here. The world has changed beyond anything I dare to know. I wouldn't have a clue what to do or where to go. The peace and quiet suits me. I'm sure I am not the only dragon who wants to stay hidden.'

'Then how come we are here?' said Finn.

'Because I called you.' replied the dragon.

Both children looked at each other, '.... you called us?' they said at once, hardly believing what the dragon had just said.

'How...why....what do you mean?' said Jess.

Finn looked at the dragon suspiciously. 'You left that note on the balloon in the field, didn't you? The note was signed A at the bottom. A for Athelstan. You put the treasure map in the book in Buckland Farm.'

'Yes, young Finn, you are right. I did write the note on the balloon and place the map in Buckland Farm. I stole that page out of the ancient book two hundred years ago on my night of freedom. I have kept it safe down here waiting for a hundred years to pass. The last full moon before this one, I was able to escape from the woodland and walked as a free man into the fields under the moonlight. You do not know how good it feels to be in the open air after having been surrounded by trees for all that time. I made my way to Buckland Farm, there has always been a farmhouse there, ever since I was baron of this land. I placed the map in the book and set the note on an old balloon I had found in the woods.'

Finn looked pleased and surprised at the dragon's answer, but he wanted to know one more thing.

'I just have one more question if that is okay. Why did you call us?'

The dragon gave a slight nod of understanding and his eyes became brighter. 'Now we get to the heart of things.' He raised his head and gave the impression that he had thought about this moment for a long time.

'There are many reasons why I have called you and Jess to find me... I have watched the world turn and time pass for hundreds of years from this woodland. Time teaches us many lessons. It helps us gain knowledge and understanding of what is important. I have seen the world change from generation to generation. I have learnt the hard way that happiness does not come from gaining more. I have often thought, what would have happened to me had I managed to escape with the treasure that stormy night? I know now that all I would have wanted is more treasure and more power but it would never have made me happy. I would never find peace. Time has taught me to value the simple things in life. Those are the real treasures. You ask why I have called you two to me, it is very simple. I want to teach you what is important in life. You are both young and have the chance to learn the secret of what real treasure is. I want to teach you how to look for magic in what you do every day. It is all around you, you just have to look for it. I have seen you grow up on the farm and know that you both have a good hearts.' The dragon paused and a look of sadness came into his eyes.

'There are those who are blinded to these treasures. I have learnt that greed traps a man. It is like drinking from a cup and never feeling refreshed. Life for them is all about greed and wanting more. There is a local family who claim to own these woods. The Cramner family have been looking for the lost treasure for countless generations. They want it all for themselves.' Finn and Jess looked at each other at the mention of Cramner.

Finn thought to himself, that is why Farmer Cramner is always in the woods. He is looking to find the treasure. No wonder he didn't want anyone else going near the castle. He is worried someone else will find it before he does.

'So young Finn and Jess, I thank you for being brave and coming to find me. I hope my words make sense to you both and I hope.... we can be friends.'

The dragon nodded his head again and blinked slowly. He had told the children his reasons for calling them to him and this gave him peace. Finn and Jess were held in that moment. They understood that what they had been told by the dragon was more precious than any treasure they could have found under the castle. They both knew then that this was one of these moments which would live in their memories for the rest of their lives. The silence stretched out amongst them and Jess could feel the magic fizzing in the air.

The silence was broken by two tiny voices coming from Finn's rucksack which was on its side where he had left it. One of the voices could be heard clearly, while the other one was muffled and not sounding very happy at all.

'What do you mean, you think you're stuck? Just climb out the way you got in,' said the tiny voice from outside the rucksack. 'No, I'm not going to help you get out. It's your fault for staying in there. I'm still finishing my lunch.... Anyway, it's your problem. And you missed Lord Athelstan of bad breath giving a very important talk to the children. How are you getting on in there?'

There came another muffled slightly louder response from inside the backpack. The top half of the backpack also started to be bounced up and down.

'No, I will not help you out, if you're going to behave like a baby mouse and have a tantrum then fine. It was your fault for wanting to have your lunch inside the backpack. All because you thought you would get more if you stayed inside it. From what Athelstan has just told the children, it all seems to make sense about people who are greedy.

From the backpack came even more muffled noise and a lot more bouncing took place.

'It's your problem you've eaten too much and you're now too fat to get out through the hole. I would stop jumping up and down if I were you, otherwise you will feel sick.'

'What's that.... you do feel sick, oh great, that's just what we need.'

There was silence from the backpack before a very strange, muffled noise could be heard and then silence again.

Jess turned around and smiled at the little mouse who was sitting quite comfortably on the floor with her back legs crossed in front of her, munching on a bit of Finn and Jess's sandwich that she held between her front paws. The mouse stopped eating immediately mid mouthfull when she realised Jess was looking at her. She looked up at the gigantic figure of Jess.

'Hello', said Jess. Now, if you were to say to Jess, when she woke up that morning, that she would be having a conversation with a talking mouse who was busy eating her picnic. Jess would have thought you were mad; but having met and now befriended a dragon. Jess realised that anything was possible when magic is involved.

'Oh, hello.' said the mouse finishing her mouthful looking rather embarrassed. 'I don't suppose you could help my friend out, could you? She seems to have got herself stuck in the rucksack. I think the hole she crawled in by is a now a bit too small for her. I apologise for eating your food and for the mess she's made. It's .... Well.... it's what we mice do.'

'Of course,' said Jess as she smiled some more and bent down to open the zip on the rucksack so the other mouse could escape.

'Oh thank you....thank you....you are so kind,' babbled the other mouse as it half fell, half rolled out of the rucksack onto the floor. It tried to stand up and give a bow but its tummy was so full, it couldn't quite find the balance to stay upright and toppled over.

'You look like you might have eaten too much,' giggled Jess.

'Well, yes, I have eaten possibly a little too much, I suppose. It's not every day I get to eat my own body weight in sandwiches. I would like to thank you and your brother for bringing in such a delightful picnic for us to enjoy today. It really was very kind. Do come again with more food anytime you like...maybe even tomorrow, and the next day and every day....'

The little mouse tailed off as she realised, he had probably said too much. Also, the other mouse was standing with her paws on her hips again and shaking her head.

'Oh, please don't worry, thank you for saying thank you. You are the politest mice I have ever had the pleasure of speaking to, and Finn is not my brother, he is my cousin.'

The two mice looked very happy that they weren't in any trouble for eating the food. The mouse who had rolled out of the bag with a rather round stomach then kept on trying to curtsey to Jess as if she were a royal princess. Jess found this very funny. Finn looked on and smiled.

'Athelstan, I know this is a silly question to ask at this point but how come you and the mice can talk? You're going to tell us that it is the magic of the woodland, aren't you?' It had only just occurred to him that he should have asked this much earlier but, in a way, this was the most special part of the whole adventure.

Athelstan gave what Finn would describe as a dragon smile. His eyes lit up and he looked happier.

'All animals can talk dear Finn; you just need to be in the right place to hear them. The magic in this cave makes it possible. You must have thought before now that the animals on your father's farm are talking to each other? Well, they are.'

'Wow,' said Finn as he thought about his father's cows.

The dragon continued, 'The next time you see animals together look at them, really look at them, they will be talking to each other. The next time you look deep into animals' eyes, you will see that they can talk. You just need to be in the right place to it hear them.'

Finn suddenly thought of Rocket and all she had done to protect them from the three evil dogs.

The dragon lowered his head towards him and asked as gently as a dragon could, 'Finn what is the matter, you look troubled?'

'I have just remembered my own dog Rocket, she saved us today, I so hope she is alright.' Finn sighed and looked worried. He pulled his knees up towards him and hugged himself.

The dragon lifted his head and gave what Finn could only describe as a wink with his left eye.

'I'm fine Finn, no dog is going to chase me down,' said Rocket as she padded towards them from the tunnel entrance. 'Although, if I have to run that far again, I must make sure I stop eating all the leftovers given to me by Mum.'

Finn and Jess were totally, utterly and completely lost for words. Their mouths were open but not a sound came out.

Rocket stood there in front of them; she looked tired and had scratches all over her, but she was alright.

'What, are you not going to give me a cuddle then?' she said and jumped into Finn and Jess's open arms. Tears rolled down the children's cheeks and they all laughed with complete joy.

Even the mice were crying with happiness. Well, crying would be how you describe Pee Mouse's reaction. Hysterical wailing and loud sobbing would fit better for the one with the extra round tummy.

'Rocket, how on earth did you find us? Where did you go? What happened to those nasty black dogs? I can't believe you can talk!'

Rocket eased herself down into Finn's lap and rested her head on Jess's leg. 'I have a secret to tell you Finn and Jess.' Her voice sounded just like Jess had imagined it would; it was calm and kind.

'You know yesterday when I ran off from you, well, I could feel the magic of this cave calling me. I have never been up here before to the castle but I knew that someone wanted to talk to me.' Rocket looked at the dragon. 'I found my way to the tunnel here and met Athelstan. I told him that you both were in the woods looking for the castle and so we came to find you.'

'That's what that noise was in the trees. It was you,' said Finn, looking up.

'I then raced around and met you in the field on your return. As for those other dogs, I wouldn't worry about them. They are as stupid as they look. They couldn't catch me, I lead them into the darkest part of the wood and left them there. They are probably still trying to find a way out now!'

145

Athelstan the dragon watched on and had peace. He had found three new friends that would be with him for some time. Perhaps this is what he wanted all along. This was his treasure to find.

Finn and Jess walked in a happy silence through the field back towards the farm. They were lost in their own thoughts, remembering all that they had seen and heard. Rocket bounced through the grass and smiled at them as she chased the insects.

'I've just realised why Farmer Cramner was driving down the drive to Buckland Farm that night.' said Finn. 'He must have seen the note on the balloon caught in the hedge. I saw him in the woods at the same time I saw the note. He must have read it and that is why he was there. I must have beaten him to find the map.' Finn smiled to himself as he understood what this meant.

Jess and Finn stopped halfway down the field and looked out over the farm and the beautiful countryside before them. The sun was beginning to slip from the horizon, turning the white shoelace clouds a crispy deep red.

'Are you sad that we didn't find actual treasure?' said Jess, turning towards him.

Finn carried on looking into the distance. He paused and then looked at Jess.

'No, I'm not sad. Through all this I have realised that we have so many treasures already. The problem is, we often choose not to see them. Athelstan was right, there is magic all around us, we just have to look for those moments. It's the simple things that make us happy. Like the smell of Mums cooking, snuggling in a warm duvet when it's raining outside, being brave when we are scared,'

'Playing with Rocky or building Palaces in the attic' added Jess with a twinkle in her eye.

'Exactly,' said Finn. 'There is one thing though, you know we can't tell anyone about what's happened, don't you?'

Jess nodded and understood exactly what he meant. She then charged after Rocket with a joyful squeal, skipping through the field with her arms waving around in circles.

Finn turned and looked up into the woodland. This adventure was over, but Finn knew there would be more very soon. He smiled and from deep in the hidden undergrowth a dragon smiled back.

Printed in Great Britain
by Amazon

70404889R00087